*A Labor of Love*

# A Labor of Love

MARTHA AMBROSE

Montlake Romance

The characters and events portrayed in this book are fictitious. Any similarity to real persons, living or dead, is coincidental and not intended by the author.

Text copyright © 1995 by Martha Ambrose
All rights reserved.
Printed in the United States of America.

No part of this book may be reproduced, or stored in a retrieval system, or transmitted in any form or by any means, electronic, mechanical, photocopying, recording, or otherwise, without express written permission of the publisher.

Published by Montlake Romance
P.O. Box 400818
Las Vegas, NV 89140

ISBN-13: 9781477835821
ISBN-10: 1477835822

*This title was previously published by Avalon Books; this version has been reproduced from the Avalon book archive files.*

*A Labor of Love*

# Chapter One

She was going to be late again.

Catherine Walker jammed down the gas pedal. Instead of taking off, though, her old Chrysler sedan moved forward at a slow, steady speed. She clenched her fingers around the steering wheel. This was ridiculous. She could get out and push it and move faster. But that was the kind of car she had chosen. It didn't accelerate quickly, it didn't have sleek lines or twin cam turbos, but it was safe and sturdy and dependable. It was a tank, a turtle, but the slow and steady often won the race, she reminded herself.

Catherine gradually built up speed, closing in on a van plodding along in the fast lane. As she hovered only a few feet from its rear bumper, she noticed the driver of the van was looking out his passenger window, taking in the sights. She barely restrained herself from flashing her headlights to get the van to pull over. After a few moments of drumming her fingers against the wheel, she swerved abruptly to the right, passing the offensive vehicle in front of her on the inside.

She shook her head in disbelief. *Some people think they own the road, just because they're on vacation.* She knew the winter tourists were the backbone of the southwest Florida economy, but, darn it, what were they doing poking along so early in the morning?

1

"Some of us have jobs to get to," Catherine muttered under her breath as she moved out in front of the van. She anxiously checked the clock on the dashboard. Eight forty-five. She had fifteen minutes to get to that all-important meeting with her boss. She'd get there on time if she had to push her sedan to the breaking point and cut off every tourist in the vicinity.

*Don't get a speeding ticket,* a tiny voice whispered inside. She'd already had one this year, and it had caused a hefty hike in her insurance rates.

Her glance flicked down at the speedometer. Sixty miles per hour. She was only doing ten miles over the limit. Maybe she'd make it in time. She almost groaned in frustration when she saw the fuel light flashing red. No! The tank couldn't possibly be empty yet; she'd just filled it a few days ago. She checked the gauge. Sure enough, it registered empty.

A wild thought ran through her mind. Maybe she should keep on going, try to make it to work. But if she ran out of gas, she'd be lucky if she got to work by lunch. *Calm down,* she thought as she took in a couple of steadying breaths.

Catherine reluctantly lifted her foot off the gas pedal, slowing down so she could turn into the gas station just ahead. She quickly pulled up to the pumps, checking her watch. Ten minutes. She had ten minutes to have her tank filled and get to work. She shoved a stray strand of honey-blond hair behind her ear. Today just wasn't going to happen the way she'd planned. Nothing was working according to schedule, and she hated that. Even with all her organized planning, nothing was going right that morning.

When no one materialized to fill her tank, she turned her head to the right and then left, searching for someone—anyone!—but there was no one in sight. Suddenly, her glance zeroed in on an attendant in jeans and a white shirt. His back was toward her and he was leaning against the gas pump, apparently just daydreaming. She sighed in exasperation. A space cadet. Just what she needed.

Catherine quickly rolled down her window. "Do you mind?" she ripped out the words impatiently.

The man didn't move; he just continued staring off into the distance.

"Hey! I'd like you to do your job if you can spare the time," Catherine said in an even louder and more annoyed tone.

The man slowly turned around. He looked at her with a languid expression. "Were you talking to me?" he asked politely.

She laughed, and there was a little hysteria in her voice. "Do you see anyone else around here?" She gestured in an arc with her right hand.

He strolled toward her car. Catherine's eyes widened as he approached and she saw how tall and broad-shouldered he was. Nervously, she checked her watch again, then continued in a frosty voice, "Look, I'm late for work, so could you fill my tank so I can at least get there by quitting time?"

As she turned to hand him her credit card, she found herself staring up into the darkest, warmest brown eyes she'd ever seen. The man had placed his arms against the roof of her car and was lounging nonchalantly against her door. He was also smiling in a way that seemed particularly irritating to Catherine.

"Seems like you need to slow down a little, ma'am," he drawled, emphasizing the last word with exaggerated politeness.

"I beg your pardon?" Catherine blinked in surprise, her irritation momentarily forgotten.

"Slow down. Wherever you're going will still be there, no matter what time you arrive." He turned up his smile a notch, revealing a small indentation on his left cheek.

How could a man so big and muscled suddenly look boyish because of a dimple in his cheek?

3

"If I don't make this meeting at Palm City Community College, President Cramer will be furious. Since I've had this job less than a year, I—" Catherine stopped abruptly. Why was she explaining herself to this perfect stranger? And a gas station attendant, no less. Her mother would have been horrified that she'd even spoken to a "service person," as she had delicately referred to them. But her mother had probably never seen one with rock-hard shoulders and melting sable eyes, Catherine thought wryly.

His smile was so engaging, Catherine found herself struggling to maintain her rigid composure. "Just fill the tank, please," she said shortly.

The man's dark eyes ran over her features again. "Too much tension—it shows in your face. Life's too short to go around being tense all the time. And you're too young and gorgeous to have frown lines already."

Frown lines? Catherine glanced over at the rearview mirror to check. Sure enough, a tiny furrow had appeared between her brows, and the corners of her mouth seemed set in a downward curve. Anxiously, she checked her shoulder-length fall of blond hair for any trace of gray.

*Come on, you're only twenty-nine,* she reminded herself.

What next? First she's late and now she's got some gas station guru telling her she needs to slow down and smell the flowers.

"Okay, fine. I'm late, I'm tense, and I'm going to be a wrinkled mess by the time I'm forty. But just what do I have to do to get my tank filled?" she sputtered, bristling with indignation.

"Are you always this much fun in the morning?" he countered. The lively twinkle in his eye only incensed her more.

"I just want some gas," she almost shouted.

"Just a minute, lady," a young man said as he came running toward her car.

Catherine looked beyond the handsome devil lounging in her window to the tall, skinny boy with straight brown hair falling in his face who was now standing by her car. "Sorry, ma'am, I was working on an engine," he apologized. "Fill it up?"

Catherine nodded and handed him her credit card wordlessly. How could she have been so stupid? She felt the heat rising to her face as her glance shifted back to the man, who stared back in waiting silence.

For a long moment, she looked at him. Then the corners of her mouth started to curve up into a smile before she could stop herself.

"That's more like it," he said, his dark eyes lingering on the peachy gloss of Catherine's lips. "And just for the sight of that smile, I'll wash your windshield."

A silvery laugh floated up from Catherine's throat. Who was this man? He was impudent, charming, and just too darn good-looking for his own good. How could any man have hair that thick and dark, curling in a rakish way just above his collar? Catherine shook her head slightly. She had to get control of this situation again. She prided herself on being a coolheaded administrator who never let her guard down. But everything had been turned upside-down this morning when the alarm clock hadn't gone off. With all her careful planning last night for this meeting, she couldn't believe she had forgotten to set the alarm.

She cleared her throat and began in the formal voice she reserved for meetings, "My apologies. I'm afraid I made a snap judgment about you. It's just that I *am* in a bit of a hurry."

"So you said." He deftly pulled the squeegee across her wet windshield.

"Right." She watched the flexing muscles in his arms in fascination. Obviously, whoever this man was, he was too insensitive to accept her attempts to ease her own embarrassment. He wasn't wearing a business suit, so he probably wasn't used to dealing with professional women. In fact, he didn't appear to understand the etiquette of conversation at all.

Mercifully, the real attendant returned with Catherine's credit slip for the gas. She hurriedly signed the slip, hoping her unwanted intruder hadn't noted the tremor in her hand as he approached her door.

"Thank you," she said brusquely as she received her copy back from the young man. She leaned forward and turned the key to start her engine, hoping the other man would step away from her car.

He slowly straightened up and lightly tapped the roof of her car. "Drive safely. And take it easy. Life's too short to—"

"Thanks for the window wash." *The lecture I could do without. Talk about condescending.* But as she drove away, she couldn't help glancing in the rearview mirror. As if sensing her interest, he waved his hand in a saluting gesture. Catherine blinked and couldn't help a rueful laugh. That had to be the most bizarre encounter with a stranger that she'd had in a long time—and one that wasn't completely disagreeable, she had to admit to herself. For a moment, she had the sudden desire to turn the car around and at least ask him his name.

Catherine laughed at her own foolishness this time. He wasn't her type at all. She needed someone who was stable, businesslike, and ambitious. Someone who would help her get ahead in her career, not someone who would slow her down. Someone who wanted more out of life than—Oh, no! Catherine looked down at her watch. It was nine o'clock. She floored the gas pedal.

～

By the time Catherine reached her office, she was fifteen minutes late and a nervous wreck.

# A Labor of Love

"He's waiting for you in his conference room," her secretary, Marilyn, said in a low voice. She handed Catherine a cup of coffee and a manila folder. Marilyn, in her mid-forties with a trim figure and perfectly styled cap of silver-gray hair, was the perfect assistant. She was cool and efficient and, what's more, she didn't expect the two of them to be friends. Marilyn just did her job—thank goodness. Catherine didn't have time for anything else.

"What's the boss's temperature in there?" Catherine asked with some trepidation as she took a deep gulp of the coffee.

"So cold you could hang meat." Marilyn placed her arms around herself and acted out an imaginary shiver.

"Oh, boy." Catherine tried not to grimace as she took another swallow of coffee. The president of the college did not like to be kept waiting, especially by his vice-president of academic affairs. "Did you include the report on faculty development?" She tapped the manila folder with her fingers as she headed toward the conference room.

"It's in there," Marilyn said as she opened the door and deftly retrieved Catherine's coffee cup.

As Catherine slipped past her, a tiny flicker of hope stirred in her breast. Maybe the president wouldn't be all that annoyed with her. After all, *he* was habitually late for his meetings.

Once the door closed, however, and Catherine's glance zeroed in on the president's ramrod-straight back, whatever hope she had entertained of conciliation dissolved. She quickly walked around the conference table, noting the staccato motion of his pen tapping up and down on a large yellow legal pad.

"Do you realize that I have been waiting ten minutes?" he asked in a tense, clipped voice.

"Yes, sir, and I apologize." She slid into one of the leather chairs across the table from him, feeling the chill emanating from his forbidding glance even at that distance. She folder her hands on top of the manila folder and waited for him to continue. It was better not to launch into lengthy explanations—he didn't like hearing meaningless details. Besides, how could she tell him that she would have been on time, except she'd had an unexpected encounter with a handsome stranger?

"We have a difficult situation coming up here at Palm City Community College," the president said, as if addressing a formal gathering. Catherine's attention immediately snapped back as he pushed a thick folder in her direction. "As you know, the faculty voted in a union last month." His mouth thinned in irritation at the word "union." Other than that slight betrayal of emotion, his expression was the familiar blank mask Catherine had come to know.

With his waving gray hair and tanned face, President Cramer was still a handsome man even though he was in his late fifties. He might be more handsome, Catherine speculated, if he ever showed any warmth in his face. But his warmth was saved for press conferences and fund-raisers where he had to play the part of the concerned administrator.

"Yes, Dr. Cramer, I know."

"Though why the faculty needs a union, I'll never understand," he continued, tapping his pen even more impatiently.

Catherine refrained from commenting. Having been a faculty member at Palm City Community College for three years before moving into an administrative position, she was well acquainted with the dissatisfaction among her former colleagues.

"Anyway, we're stuck and now we have to deal with it. Or rather, you do." The tapping of the pen stopped.

"I do?"

He nodded. "The next step after voting in a union, obviously, is negotiating a contract. And that's where you come in," he explained. "You'll work on the contract as the management representative."

"But I've never done anything like that before. I... I thought we were going to talk about faculty development today," Catherine found herself saying before she could stop herself. "Not that I can't handle it," she amended hastily. "But it's a legal document, and I have no experience in that area."

"Our lawyers will advise you, of course. And the material in the folder"—he gestured to the thick file he had given her—"will give you some guidelines for collective negotiations."

"Will I be working with the faculty while representing management on this contract?" She didn't relish having to do that. Many of the faculty members were still friends, though she hadn't had much time to socialize with them recently.

He shook his head. "No, their affiliate union is sending in a field representative and he'll be the one you work with. No doubt he'll be a real pro at getting what he wants. I'll expect you to be equally tough at holding the line."

"I see." Translated, that meant she'd be spending many long hours in a cramped room arguing with some left-wing labor champion. She almost groaned aloud. She was busy enough as it was. But, then again, this could mean a real opportunity for her career. "When is the field rep due?"

"Today. He's supposed to meet us here at nine-thirty. I told your secretary to send him in when he arrives." President Cramer's gray eyes fastened on Catherine with the warmth of cold steel. "I don't need to tell you how important this contract is, Catherine—both for the college and you."

"Yes. I mean, no. I mean, I understand."

He paused for a few moments and then leaned back in his chair, his glance narrowing. "I'm not sure that you do. The faculty here has gotten very demanding, and we can't let them think they're going to run this college. They need to realize that this union is not going to be the springboard to unlimited power. So the contract needs to be in management's favor every step of the way."

Catherine nodded back at him without speaking.

His eyebrows flickered a little before he continued. "Your performance in the last few months has been, how should I say it, less than stellar. When I hired you almost a year ago, it wasn't only because your late mother and I had been friends, it was because I saw something in you that was special—a drive to achieve, good problem-solving skills. Those are the things that make a good administrator. But your monthly reports have been unremarkable and you've been late twice for meetings, including today," he emphasized the last word with heavy irony. "Now I know your mother died only six months ago, but you have a job to do."

A stab of pain shot through Catherine. She'd barely had time to mourn her mother's death, much less get a handle on this job. But that's how her mother would've wanted it. In fact, she had wanted Catherine to get this job more than Catherine herself had wanted it. Her mother's ambitions for her had been limitless, and Catherine wouldn't have put it past her mother to try everything in her power to convince President Cramer to promote her to vice-president.

An even deeper and more familiar pain tugged at her with this thought. Her mother had never been interested in the things that other mothers were—such as seeing her daughter happy, maybe even married with a couple of kids. Catherine's career had been the only thing that the two of them could ever really talk about. They never gossiped about friends or spent the afternoon shopping. Instead, her mother obsessed over every aspect of Catherine's path to becoming a successful executive.

At least her mother had lived to see the big promotion. She had been able to see Catherine become vice-president. As for her father, well. ... Pressing her lips together in a determined line,

Catherine squarely met the president's glance. "I know I've been off the pace a little, but I won't let you down on this contract. You can count on me."

"I hope so, Catherine," he said with a lethal calmness. "A lot is riding on these contract negotiations. I expect you to fight hard for the administration's position. In fact, I expect you to fight as if your job depended on it."

Catherine's throat suddenly went dry. Was he saying this was her last chance to show she had what it took to be an administrator? This assignment was going to be difficult enough without feeling like her job was hanging in the balance.

The door to the conference room swung open and both pairs of eyes fastened on Marilyn and the man who was with her. Dr. Cramer's glance was cold and Catherine's was incredulous. Neither look was lost on the newcomer.

"This is Michael Moreno, the field representative from the American Federation of Teachers," Marilyn announced as Catherine and the president rose from their chairs. No one noticed as Marilyn closed the door and quickly disappeared.

Michael walked forward, extending his hand to the president. "Dr. Cramer, I've looked forward to meeting you."

As they shook hands, the president inclined his head toward Catherine. "This is Catherine Walker. She's the VP for academic affairs and she'll be the one working closely with you on the contract."

"It's a pleasure," Michael turned toward her, his face registering no emotion other than an impersonal friendliness, but Catherine detected a slight twinkle in those irreverent brown eyes.

She stiffened, conscious of fate's warped sense of humor. This was unbelievable! How could the man she'd met at the gas station less than an hour ago suddenly turn up as the union representative? He was now wearing a lightweight navy blazer with his jeans, but it was the same man. The same firm jaw and curling black hair around his collar. The same solid shoulders, the same laconic smile.

With a tremendous effort, she fought to pull herself together. "How do you do?" Her hand was caught in his firm grip and the contact sent waves of warmth up her arm. She quickly withdrew her hand, glancing at the president, but he seemed oblivious to the undercurrents between her and Michael.

"Mr. Moreno, I'll leave the two of you to decide how you want to proceed," the president was saying. "You can hammer out the details of your working arrangement, but management would like to see a draft of the contract in four to six weeks."

"That seems reasonable," Michael replied. He hoisted a worn leather briefcase onto the conference table. Papers were sticking out of it at odd angles. "I'm ready to get started whenever you are, Ms. Walker."

The president was nodding in approval. "That's what I like—action. But I warn you, Mr. Moreno, Catherine will be a tough negotiator. You're going to have your work cut out for you if you're expecting a lot of concessions from her."

"One can always hope," Michael came back.

Catherine was cringing inside. This was sounding worse and worse. She'd be spending six weeks negotiating with a man whom she'd ordered around like a lackey at the gas station. "Would you like to stay for the ground rules session, Dr. Cramer?" she asked hopefully.

"No need. This is your project now." The president started out of the room. "But I'll expect progress reports, of course," he added before he made an exit.

Silence descended like a heavy blanket over the room.

Michael's admiring gaze traveled over Catherine's trim figure, revealed by her soft yellow suit. The skirt ended just above the knees, showing her slim legs to advantage.

# A Labor of Love

His glance came to rest on her flushed face. Those finely chiseled, patrician features were delicately tinted pink as though an artist had brushed them with the softest of pastels. She was embarrassed and he knew he should say something to ease her embarrassment. But it was a good negotiating tactic to put the other side on the defensive.

He had recognized her this morning at the gas station from her picture in the college catalog that was in his file. He had intended to introduce himself, but when she started barking out the orders, he couldn't resist playing with her a little. And now he could use her discomfort to his advantage. Somehow, though, that thought made him uncomfortable. He didn't like to play on people's weaknesses when negotiating a contract, even if the opposition was a bit on the haughty side.

"Shall we sit down?" he began in a friendly tone.

Catherine slid into a chair, still not looking at him.

As Michael seated himself across the table from her, he noted the vulnerable curve to her lower lip. Maybe she wasn't as sure of herself as she pretended to be. "Look, perhaps we need to clear the air first, or we're not going to be able to get anywhere," he was saying.

Catherine held up a hand, struggling for the right words. "I don't know what to say, except I'm sorry. I was in a hurry this morning, and I thought you were the attendant."

"I know."

"But I didn't mean to...slight you in any way."

"Of course not."

"I'm normally more patient than that."

"I'm sure you are."

Her blue eyes fastened on his brown ones. Was he mocking her? A sudden disturbing thought occurred to her. Was that encounter a tactic meant to put her on the defensive? Had he engineered that meeting at the gas station? No. He couldn't have known she'd be there. But she couldn't let him continue with the upper hand. Her job may well be at risk. "Well, then." Catherine took in a deep breath. "Now that's out in the open, maybe we can get down to business, Mr. Moreno."

"Sounds good. Why don't you call me Mike, and I'll call you Katie?" he suggested. That disturbing light was back in his eyes. She'd show him that she wasn't some novice at the negotiating game, even if she hadn't done a union contract before.

Catherine smiled smoothly as she leaned her elbows on the table. "Why don't I call you Mr. Moreno, and you call me Ms. Walker?"

Michael gave a short bark of laughter. "Whatever you say, *Ms. Walker.*"

Catherine didn't care much for his tone, and she surely didn't like the way these negotiations were beginning. This was serious business, and Michael Moreno was much too flippant. She also didn't like the assessing way he'd looked at her. It made her uncomfortable. "Again, I don't mean to offend, but since this *is* a negotiation between two opposing sides, it would be better if we kept the whole thing on a professional level."

"It doesn't have to be antagonistic, though," Michael pointed out. He continued on a more serious note, "I've found in these situations, when an initial contract is being drafted, that if both sides work together in a friendly atmosphere, they get better results."

"I completely agree," Catherine said, feeling somewhat mollified. "But the degree of friendliness is in question."

His disarming grin made light of her concern. "I prefer informality."

"That's obvious."

"Is it? Because I'm not dressed in a three-piece suit?" he said wryly.

"Well, a suit is what a person would normally wear to a meeting like this." Not a jacket with jeans. That definitely wasn't appropriate.

"Suits are often used to mask the shark that lies within," he corrected. "Some of us prefer it a little more honest."

"So you show your fins at the first meeting?" she retorted.

"Only if they need to surface." His dark eyebrows arched mischievously.

"I...I think we need to talk about the ground rules," she said hurriedly to change the subject. She would not let herself get caught up in sparring with this man. That could distract her, and being around him would be distracting enough without playing word games.

"I agree," he said, flipping open his briefcase. "I brought along sample copies of ground rules that I've used in other negotiations." He handed her the copies. "As you can see, they suggest that we come to mutual agreement on times and places for meetings, that we keep records of the meetings, and that we sign off on sections as we come to agreement."

Catherine scanned over the sheet. "I'll look it over tonight and see if there's anything I want to add or delete, but it appears to be acceptable."

"Do you want to add a 'suit' clause?" he asked with mock severity.

Catherine refused to rise to his bait. She leaned forward, her chin resting on her knuckles. "I don't think that's necessary. You can wear whatever you want, Mr. Moreno. You can even wear shorts if you want. It really doesn't matter as long as you keep in mind that we're here to settle this contract, and that's all."

"Fine. Just as long as you don't ask me to fill your gas tank."

Irritated, Catherine immediately straightened in her chair. "I thought I'd already explained that little episode and we agreed to forget it."

"Maybe *you* did," he drawled. "But I'm still not certain you're seeing me as an equal unless I conform to your expectations of how I should look and dress." He paused, smiling. "And I have no intention of doing that. So, I guess I need some reassurances."

"Like what?" She sensed an ulterior motive.

Here was his chance to gain the upper hand with her. He didn't like these mind games, but it was his job. "Like you're willing to let me have an office on campus that could then be used as a union office after I'm gone."

He watched as Catherine looked down at her hands clasped tightly on the table. She appeared to be thinking over his proposition. It would be a major tactical gain to assert the union's presence on the campus so early in the negotiations. Catherine's shoulders began to shake, and Michael's anticipation turned to puzzlement. As she glanced up again, he saw that her lips were trembling from the need to laugh. "I'll give you an A for effort on that one, Mr. Moreno. It was original and even gets points for sincerity," she joked.

He bowed his head in acknowlegement. "You can't blame a negotiator for trying."

"I sure don't," she said, as she gained control over herself again. This was all part of the negotiations. He might have been offended by her behavior this morning, but he was also trying to turn it to his advantage. He had a lot to learn if he thought she was that naive.

His brown eyes kindled in admiration. "Looks like we're going to have some stimulating sessions ahead."

Catherine smiled blandly. "I'm ready for whatever you throw my way."

"Is that a challenge. Ms. Walker?"

"Just a fact, Mr. Moreno."

"I might have one or two curves up my sleeve."

"That's the way you play the game, isn't it?"

Michael studied her for a few moments. The sparkling blue eyes and soft blond hair that fell to her shoulders couldn't have been more feminine. But her chin jutted out with the determination of someone who was used to winning. Strength and intelligence were apparent in every aspect of her presence.

He could hardly wait for their next meeting—and not only to work on the contract. This was one woman he wanted to get to know better.

Michael was nodding. "It should be an interesting game—for both of us."

# Chapter Two

It took Catherine most of the afternoon to recover from her meeting with Michael Moreno. She kept replaying portions of their conversation in her head, but she rephrased her parts so she had the verbal upper hand at every step of the way. In her imaginary recreation of their conversation, she bested him with her wit and intelligence to the point that he became almost tongue-tied.

"This has got to stop," she told herself firmly as she turned down the street to her house and caught herself still indulging in those imaginary comebacks. She and Michael had agreed that they would meet tomorrow at ten o'clock for their first meeting and, until then, she should just put him out of her mind.

As Catherine pulled into the driveway, she felt none of the usual calm at the sight of the house she grew up in. Michael had thrown her off balance, and even the security and familiarity of her home didn't relieve the tension inside her. Normally, she was soothed by the sight of her Spanish-style stucco house with the massive jacaranda tree spread across the front yard. But not tonight.

Built in an older section of town in the 1930s, her house resembled many of the others built at that time, but hers had a small second story that resembled a tower on one side of the house. That was her bedroom. It had been a storage room when her mother was alive, but, after she died, Catherine had a bathroom added and turned the space into a cozy bedroom. An ivory tower—that's what her neighbor, Ruth Rigby, called it.

Hardly that, Catherine thought wryly. She'd had the whole house painted a warm salmon color two months ago—a far cry from its former neutral beige. Mother would be aghast at the sight of it, Catherine realized. But she would be overjoyed at how the neighborhood was suddenly being rediscovered as a historical area. The young professionals in town wanted a piece of history and they were willing to pay large sums for the privilege of owning and fixing up one of the old houses. How ironic that the neighborhood's old-fashioned, rundown reputation that so distressed her mother was being replaced by the idea that this was *the* place to live once again.

All the houses sparkled with new stucco and fresh paint. The lawns were carefully manicured and the citrus trees were meticulously trimmed. Brand-new luxury cars were parked in the driveways. The old neighborhood was definitely looking upper-class, which suited Catherine to a tee.

*But just because I like things to look nice doesn't mean I'm the snob that Michael obviously thinks I am,* Catherine reassured herself. *I like things to be neat, but they don't have to be perfect.*

Just the thought of him caused her thoughts to drift back to the conference room again and, distracted once more, Catherine jammed on the brakes just in time to keep her sedan from hitting the back wall of the carport. She sighed and shook her head at her own foolishness. "One more day like this and I'll be reduced to a blithering idiot," she muttered as she grabbed her overstuffed briefcase and headed for the front door.

"Cutting that a bit close, huh?" her neighbor, Ruth, called over.

"I'll say," Catherine said as she bent to pick up her morning newspaper. She threw it in the recycling bin, unread, with the other ones from this week. She knew she should cancel her subscription, but she kept hoping she'd get around to actually start reading the paper.

"Here, take some of these, Cathy," Ruth said as she marched over with an armload of oranges. Even though Ruth Rigby was in her early seventies, she still had the trim figure and energy of the physical education teacher she'd been. It was even more fortunate that she had a straight back, since her favorite Himalayan cat, Shalimar, liked riding on her shoulders. "I just picked them so they're fresher than anything you'd get at the grocery store."

"You aren't going to stockpile these until the packing plant men come?" Catherine asked with a little smile, knowing about the special place where Ruth stored her oranges and grapefruits.

Ruth looked over at her twenty-nine-year-old Cadillac, which was parked under her carport. The back seat held a giant pile of grapefruit and the front seat bore an equally large pile of oranges. "Nope, the car is just about filled." Shalimar wrapped her long tail around Ruth's neck in contented agreement.

Catherine's features softened into amusement as her glance moved to Ruth's car. How many times growing up had she heard the story about how Ruth and her husband had bought the car new and driven it to southwest Florida to start their new life? It had always intrigued Catherine as a little girl, because the car had been made the same year that she was born. Ruth never drove the car now, so, with her usual practicality, she used it to store the oranges and grapefruits that she sold to the citrus packing plant.

"Seems like you're working a bit too hard, honey," Ruth pointed out, her still-sharp gray eyes deepening with concern.

"So what else is new?" Catherine tried to toss the comment off lightly, but it came out sounding sarcastic.

"With the kind of job you've got, Cathy, you've got to *make* time for yourself. You remember how hard my poor Tom worked at the packing plant?" Ruth paused, struggling with her emotions.

Catherine knew that even after eight years the thought of Tom's death still upset Ruth. "He thought the place would close down without him. And look what happened. He had a heart attack and died, and the packing plant is still going strong." Shalimar whined, as if in sympathy with her beloved owner.

A tug of emotion pulled at Catherine's heart. Tom had been like a father, since her own had taken off when she was too young to remember, and his death still brought a lump to her throat as well. "I know, Ruth." She patted her neighbor on the shoulder, tears threatening behind her own eyelids.

Ruth shook herself firmly. "I'm not talking about Tom. I've accepted his death. I'm talking about you, Cathy. You haven't even noticed that it's almost summer. Time for picnics at the beach, swimming, sailing—all the things you used to love to do."

"If I just had the time." Catherine sighed loudly.

"You've got *to find* the time," Ruth's voice hardened. "You could work twenty-four hours a day on the kind of job you have. But that doesn't fill your life, not really. You still come home to an empty house." Ruth fell silent for a few moments and then continued in a more gentle tone. "I'm sorry, Cathy, I shouldn't have spoken so sharply. It's just that I care so much. You're like my own daughter and I don't want to see you miss out on the kind of full life I've had. I know I wasn't able to have children, but I had a wonderful life with Tom. And I'll tell you there's some energy left in this old girl yet." Ruth's brows arched in an air of determination. "I'm not ready to turn into a crazy cat lady living alone for the rest of her life."

Catherine reached out and grasped Ruth's hand tightly. The bond between them ran deeply. "There's nothing to be sorry about. Everything you say comes from the heart, and you've got a heart of gold. Besides, I appreciate your honesty." Maybe Ruth was right about working too hard. But then Catherine immediately suppressed the thought. There was nothing wrong with driving yourself for the right type of goals. A little ambition never hurt anybody.

"By the way, did you rent your room yet?" Catherine asked, trying to change the subject. As well-meaning as Ruth was, Catherine didn't even have time to *think* about summer picnics, much less partake of them.

"Oh, my gosh." Ruth immediately dropped Catherine's hand as she raised her fingers to her mouth in dismay. "I almost forgot. A prospect called about it and is coming over in about thirty minutes. And I haven't even straightened up."

"Gee, I wish I had time to help you—"

Ruth shook her head as she dumped the oranges in Catherine's already brimming briefcase. She pulled Shalimar off her shoulder and firmly jammed her under her arm. "I can handle it."

"I better come over later and check this person out," Catherine suggested in a mock-serious voice. "We can't have just anyone moving into our neighborhood now it's getting so ritzy." She waved her hand in an exaggeratedly expansive circle.

"Oh, yeah? Well, just wait 'til I start grazing my goat. I'm getting darn tired of having to pay someone to mow this lawn," Ruth threatened.

Catherine's laugh spun out in a delighted trill. "Uh oh. There goes the neighborhood."

Later, when Catherine sat in her kitchen peeling one of Ruth's oranges for dinner, her neighbor's words filtered back through Catherine's mind. Was she right? Had Catherine been working too hard? True, she felt so drained at the end of the day, sometimes she barely had the energy to scrape off her makeup and fall into bed. Yes, she did bring piles of paperwork home at the end of the day, but that was the price she had to pay for the kind of prestige and salary her job offered. Besides, when her probationary year was almost up, things would probably ease up for her.

Only if she was able to bring the contract negotiations to successful completion, a tiny voice reminded her. Otherwise, the idea of her working too much would probably be a moot point. She wouldn't have a job at all. She shuddered inwardly at the thought. It had taken her too long to get to where she was to lose it all now. There was a sourness in the pit of her stomach, and it had nothing to do with the orange.

She'd never felt this kind of stress when she was a faculty member. She loved planning her classes, grading the papers, preparing exercises—and she had so many friends. Now, one by one, they had fallen away or, rather, Catherine had fallen away because she didn't have the time to work them into her busy schedule. Except for Linda. They had taught English together and, even though Catherine was no longer a faculty member, the two of them still met every Wednesday morning for breakfast.

That was tomorrow, Catherine mused. Maybe Linda could fill in some background about Mr. Michael Moreno. Not that Catherine was using her friend. She just wanted more information. The thought brought a tiny smile to Catherine's face. She had her sources too. And she'd be getting the upper hand on Michael next time they met.

The doorbell rang as Catherine was popping the last bite of orange in her mouth. That had to be Ruth with her new tenant. She carefully wiped her hands on a linen napkin before smoothing down her knee-length white cotton shorts and making for the door. Ruth needed the extra money, so Catherine hoped this one would stay more than two weeks. Of course, Ruth's menagerie of cats wasn't everyone's cup of tea. Catherine smiled as she remembered Ruth's last elderly renter leaving in a huff after Hovie, the black tabby, had jumped on her while she was in the shower. The woman had run out of the house screaming, wearing nothing but a towel.

Catherine's smile widened, remembering the picture of Ruth shaking the woman in front of her house, trying to snap her out of her delirium.

The smile quickly vanished as Catherine swung open her heavy oak front door, revealing Ruth and Michael Moreno. What was *he* doing here? At her house of all places!

"Cathy, isn't this delightful? Look who my new tenant turned out to be?" Ruth exclaimed. "When Michael found out you lived next door, he couldn't believe it. And you two met only this morning, he says. What a coincidence."

"Coincidence?" Catherine echoed in a wary voice.

"It certainly is my good fortune," Michael added, his dark eyes sparkling wickedly.

"And my good fortune too," Ruth added. "Michael just pulled Shalimar out from under your house again, Cathy. Why that cat goes under there and won't come out is just beyond me. Thank goodness Michael is here now and you won't have to go under there again to get Shalimar. Yessir, I call that good fortune."

*And my bad fortune,* Catherine fumed silently. How had he arranged this little deal? The man had absolutely no scruples. "Are you sure you don't want to stay at a hotel? You probably won't be in town all that long."

"Cathy, don't be silly," Ruth remonstrated her.

Catherine's hands clenched at her sides. And she was even more irritated that he showed up here when she was wearing casual attire. Even though her shorts were of a modest length and her red and white striped T-shirt was neatly pressed, it was a far cry from the professional image she wanted to convey.

Michael shrugged. "I don't like empty, sterile hotel rooms," he said, daring her to say more.

Catherine pressed her lips tightly together. She wouldn't give him the satisfaction of seeing her thrown off balance by his presence.

"I agree," Ruth said firmly. "Being with friends is always so much nicer."

Michael's mouth turned up on one side in a lopsided smile at the word "friend." Catherine's mouth turned down. She had to say something before Ruth got the wrong idea. "I'm afraid that Michael and I aren't exactly what you would call friends, Ruth."

"That's right," Michael agreed readily.

Catherine eyed him warily.

"We're more like civilized adversaries," he was saying, "because we have to settle this union contract, you see. But it doesn't mean that we're enemies, either. Right, Cathy?"

As Ruth turned to her, Catherine eked out a small "Right," not missing his use of her nickname. If he thought he was going to wheedle his way into her confidence, he had another thing coming. She wasn't born yesterday.

"Let me run back and get the rental contract, Michael. I won't be a minute." Ruth turned to Catherine. "Why don't you show him your house, Cathy? It's practically a mirror of mine, except it has the tower on the left side. And it's cleaner." She gave a parting glance over Catherine's shoulder at the stacks of papers and magazines. "Well, sort of."

Catherine gave Michael a long, hard look and then reluctantly swung her door open for him to come in. "It's really nothing special," she said in a flat tone.

As Michael strolled into the large, cool living room, his gaze moved from the shining hardwood floor to the white-washed walls, to the heavy beams in the ceiling. Anywhere but on the long-legged, slim figure of Catherine Walker. When he saw her standing in the doorway a few minutes ago, he'd found himself unable to do anything but stare at her like a love struck teenager.

Certainly her outfit was anything but deliberately provocative. It was downright conservative compared to the cutoffs and skimpy crop tops that many women wore. But with her sleek fair hair curving to her shoulders like a shimmering curtain of gold and her smooth skin glowing almost translucent, her beauty suddenly seemed softer, more approachable. There was certainly a marked difference from the severe professional he'd met this morning, he mused.

Noting his pretended interest in her house, Catherine passed him, determined to point out every feature of her home. "This fireplace, you'll notice, is very unusual, even for houses built in the thirties. It's more Victorian with the carved marble mantle."

"Matches the romantic tower, huh?" he answered, his eyes still drifting back to her. Maybe this wasn't such a good idea to live next door. Linda Fisher, from the faculty, had told him about the room for rent— and she'd let it drop that Catherine lived next door. He had raced over, thinking that it would keep Catherine a little off center for the negotiations, having him living so near. But now he realized maybe *he* would be the one made off center by her proximity.

"There's nothing romantic about the tower. It's just a room," she explained matter-of-factly. Actually, it was the one place where she felt she could drop the carefully cultivated image of the professional and relax. In her bedroom retreat, no one could see that she too had her moments of self-doubt and feelings of loneliness.

"Could I see it?"

"I don't think so. You see, it's my bedroom now, and it's a little messy. Maybe some other time I'll give you the full tour." She wrapped her arms around herself defensively. That was her private area and she had no intention of sharing it with anyone, especially

Michael Moreno. Besides, why was he being so inquisitive about her house? Was he trying to find some kind of information to use against her, or was he just being plain nosy?

"Maybe some other time," he echoed.

"Maybe," she echoed back. As she watched him through narrowed eyes, a thought suddenly occurred to her. "You know, it's a very peculiar coincidence that you just lucked on to Ruth's rental."

"No luck about it. Your friend on the faculty, Linda Fisher, told me that Ruth had a room to rent," he tossed off nonchalantly, still looking around the room with assumed interest.

*Linda, I will kill you,* Catherine silently promised. "Did she tell you I lived next door?"

His gaze came to rest on her intently. "Would it matter if she did?"

She faltered slightly under his scrutiny. "It...it depends. If you thought it would unsettle me having you so close, then yes, it does matter."

He moved closer to where she stood in front of the fireplace. "What if I simply wanted to get to know you better? Would that unsettle you?" Standing so close, he could smell the delicate scent of roses coming from her. It was as pure and sweet as a bouquet.

Her blue eyes were cool as they met his gaze. "Unsettle me, no. Concern me, yes. There's really no need for us to get to know each other personally. It could complicate things if we became—"

"Friends?"

"Well, yes. Friends would have a hard time negotiating contracts with each other." Catherine was having a hard time thinking clearly. Why was he standing so close to her? It was interfering with her normally logical way of looking at things.

"Not really," Michael answered amicably, one arm now resting comfortably across the fireplace mantle. "I like and respect many of the people I've worked on contracts with—and when a friendship develops based on mutual admiration, the negotiations move smoothly and quickly. When there are personality conflicts, the negotiations can become tedious, to say the least."

He sounded sincere enough, but she wasn't sure that she bought into his little 'I'm your friend, you're my friend' speech. It could be another trick to lull her into a false complacency. But she could play that game too. Let him think she was more gullible than she really was. "All right, Mr. Moreno, I'm willing to concede that point to you. There's certainly no need for animosity between us."

He leaned forward, smiling with satisfaction. She would be a worthy opponent, he realized. She didn't trust him any more than he trusted her, but she obviously knew when to retreat to gain a tactical advantage.

"Friends, then?" he questioned.

She nodded and extended her right hand to him.

His large palm closed over hers, lightly squeezing the soft skin of her fingers. His work-roughened skin rasped against her smooth hand. Quickly, she disengaged her hand from his, still feeling the strength and warmth of his touch.

He laughed shortly. "I guess these aren't the kind of hands you're used to." He held up his right hand and looked at both sides. The palms were callused and the skin was darkened from the sun. There were various scars that crisscrossed the back of his hand and up to his wrist. "The hands of a blue-collar worker, right?"

"That isn't what I was thinking," she protested.

"But that's what you thought at the gas station this morning," he continued, his hand dropping to his side. "Here's a guy I can order around because he's not a big-time executive. He's a nobody."

A flush crept up into Catherine's cheeks.

"Let me tell you something, Ms. Walker, an honest day's work is nothing to be ashamed of. That's why I'm a field representative for labor interests. Too many people feel like you do, that others should be ignored or looked down upon because they don't work in management jobs. They perform a valuable and necessary service. As my father used to say, 'No man is any less if he works with his hands.' And just think, if those people you try to ignore didn't do these lowly jobs, *you'd* have to do them." His voice suddenly had an intensity that caught her off guard.

"I don't ignore people," she protested again.

"But you'd like to."

"That's not true. I was a faculty member once. I know what's it's like—"

"Do you? Are you sure you haven't forgotten?"

"No, I haven't. I just have a different life now."

"One that doesn't include being nice to underlings like gas station attendants?" he insisted, a cynical edge to his voice.

With a renewed sense of embarrassment, she looked away. She couldn't let him see that he'd hit home with that last comment. Was she growing so thoughtless and self-satisfied that she wasn't aware of other people's feelings anymore? She didn't like the sound of that. She wasn't that person. This morning had just been an unusual occurrence. She'd been rushed and panicked about her meeting. "I thought we'd laid that dog to rest," she said quietly, her blue eyes a tranquil sea once more. "Friends don't keep bringing up issues that have been set aside, do they?"

"No, they don't. My apologies." *Caught in my own game,* Michael realized. He *did* want to be her friend. In fact, he wanted to be much more than that, and maybe that was the reason for his outburst. He couldn't let himself lose control like that again. What she did in her own life was her business. All he needed to

29

concern himself with was the contract. The rest was not part of the negotiations.

"So we're still on for tomorrow?" she was saying.

"What?"

"The meeting. Tomorrow at ten o'clock, right?"

"In your office, Ms. Walker."

Catherine flashed him a dazzling set of perfect, pearl-white teeth. "I think friends can be a little more informal than that, Michael."

"Katie."

"Catherine."

"Whatever."

Ruth entered Catherine's living room and immediately enthused, "Oh, I'm *so* glad to see the two of you hitting it off so well. It's obvious you both have so much in common and, being next door to each other and everything, you'll be able to see each other all the time."

The reality of Ruth's words struck Catherine like a jolt of electricity, freezing her smile.

Michael casually draped an arm around Catherine's shoulders. "Yes, I'm looking forward to Catherine and I getting to know each other."

## Chapter Three

"So what do you know about Michael Moreno?" Catherine asked, sipping her morning coffee and trying not to appear too anxious for the answer.

Linda Fisher broke out in a grin. "I was wondering when you'd get around to that."

"What do you mean?"

"Cathy, we've been having breakfast together every Wednesday for the last four years. I think I know you well enough by now to know when something's on your mind."

A wry smile turned up a corner of Catherine's mouth. "Am I so transparent?"

Linda gave a small shrug. "Only to me. And since I'm your best friend, I'll never tell."

Catherine glanced at Linda's curling red hair and clover-green eyes. There was little artifice about her friend's appearance, and she radiated a warmth and energy that practically charged anybody who came into her orbit. She was a dynamo in the classroom and the students adored her. Catherine also found her full of sound, practical sense when she needed to discuss a problem with her.

"You know I have to negotiate this union contract with him," Catherine began, nibbling on a piece of toast meditatively. "And, to tell you the truth, I'm concerned. I've never done this type of work before. But Moreno's apparently a very experienced negotiator."

"Then you just do your homework. Remember how you handled that maintenance contract bidding? You researched the companies, asked for bids, and found the one that seemed the most reliable for the money."

"But President Cramer picked the one *he* liked best from the top three," she reminded her friend. "Larry Andrews isn't the person I would have picked to handle the entire college maintenance facility." Catherine remembered how surprised she'd been when the president chose that firm.

"But the point is, you handled that deal and you can handle this one too."

"I don't know," Catherine said, biting her lower lip doubtfully. "Michael Moreno is one crafty negotiator, as well as being experienced, smart—"

"And dynamite looking?" Linda added with a mischievous sparkle in her eyes.

"Linda. You're married," Catherine cautioned.

"So? That doesn't mean I don't recognize an attractive guy when I see one." Linda gave a little wink at Catherine.

"What would Joel say?"

"Who?"

"Joel. Your husband, remember?" Catherine asked in a sarcastic tone.

"Oh, him. Well, since he's still overseas—"

"Linda!"

Linda was chuckling gently. "Oh, come on, I'm joking."

"About the good-looking part too?"

"No, not about that part—Michael *is* good-looking."

"Darn right he is." Both women burst out in spontaneous laughter. "Not that I'd notice, of course." Catherine continued in a deliberately prim voice when the laughter had subsided. "Even if he *is* going to be my new neighbor, thanks to you." She impaled her friend with a withering glance.

"Oh? Is he going to rent Ruth's room?" Linda asked in an innocent voice that didn't fool Catherine for one moment.

"What are you up to, Linda?" she asked with sudden suspicion. "You know how difficult it's going to be not only seeing him at work, but at home too."

"What's the matter? Don't trust youself?"

"Don't be ridiculous. He's not my type," Catherine assured her. "It could be...awkward, that's all."

"You just said you thought the man was attractive."

"An impartial observation."

"Now, Catherine Walker, what would Bill say?" Linda asked, a teasing smile on her face.

"You know Bill and I are just friends. We only date occasionally," Catherine pointed out a shade too defensively. Actually, she felt guilty that she hadn't given Bill a thought in the last twenty-four hours. But it was hardly like they were engaged or anything.

"Sounds safe. And boring." Linda gave an exaggerated yawn.

"Linda." Catherine warned.

"Hey, I only tell it as I see it."

"All right. All right." Catherine waved her hand in exasperation. "Enough relationship talk. We've got to be serious. This *is* serious. This contract is important."

"For the faculty too," Linda gently reminded her.

"I know that," Catherine said quietly. "I was a faculty member once too." But now the president wanted her to hold to a hard management line with this contract and, if she wanted to keep her job, she had to follow his orders. And ethically she was obligated to. But how could she tell Linda that?

Linda smiled. "I remember."

An awkward silence like an invisible wall rose up between the two women. As the waitress came and refilled their coffee mugs, Catherine glanced at her friend almost wistfully. Even though they still met and gossiped and laughed like they used to when they were both on the faculty, there was a distance between them now that Catherine had taken an administrative job. Not all that noticeable, but there nonetheless. Catherine cleared her throat lightly. "Anyway, back to Michael Moreno."

"Any day, anytime, anywhere," Linda said, her casual, jesting tone returning.

"You're awful." Catherine pretended to admonish her friend, but she was relieved that the awkwardness between them had vanished. "So what's the deal with him?"

Linda looked down at the coffee cup she held in both hands, leaning back in her chair meditatively. "I really don't know much about him, aside from the very obvious physical attributes we've both apparently noticed." Her glance shifted over to Catherine, who made a face at her. "The union sent him when we asked for an expert in contract negotiations. He has a good legal background—a law degree from Harvard—"

"What!" Catherine almost choked on her coffee.

"Yeah. Top of his class and everything. He's one smart guy."

Catherine's expression was incredulous. "With that kind of background, what's he doing working in labor law? That's not going to get him anywhere." And so much for the blue-collar act he'd been pulling on her. That was just a pretense to put her on the defensive after yesterday at the gas station. But now she knew better. She might even be able to turn this information around to *her* advantage.

"Get him anywhere?"

"You know what I mean," Catherine explained. "It's hardly the highest paying or the most prestigious area of the law."

Linda fastened a direct stare at Catherine. "Some people might think that it's one of the *best* areas of the law to practice in, because it helps others."

"I know, but—" Catherine broke off under the scrutiny of her friend. Linda was observing her with questioning eyes. "I guess I'm surprised about Moreno. Usually the Harvard law types are looking for a more high-powered kind of career." And he didn't seem like the kind of man who'd settle for second-best.

"Maybe it'll make you feel better to know he had a law practice in Miami at one time. One of those big, prestigious firms," Linda said with more than a touch of irony in her voice.

Catherine's interest quickened. "So what happened?"

"I don't know. Maybe he got tired of representing companies that try to squeeze the last drop out of their employees."

"Right," Catherine said drily. "No, there's a missing piece here and I mean to find it."

Suddenly, Linda's eyes took on a distinct gleam. "To learn more about Michael Moreno the negotiator or Michael Moreno the man? Sounds like you're more than a little interested in our field representative."

"Only in the line of duty," Catherine assured her. "The more I know about him, the better I'll be able to match his moves at the table."

"Moves? At the table?"

"Union lingo."

"I see." Linda's brows rose in amused skepticism.

"'It's true," Catherine continued. "I'm only concerned about the contract."

"I believe you. Just don't forget the little people you left behind on the faculty," Linda interjected on a more serious note. "We voted in the union because we felt we needed it for equity in our working conditions. Put yourself in our place again when you're negotiating and remember what it's like to be at the whim of management."

"You can count on me to be fair," Catherine answered in an equally serious tone. But then a sudden echo of these words flashed through her mind. Wasn't that the same thing she'd said to the president? That he could count on her. Where should her true loyalties lie? Catherine asked herself with an inward groan. The truth was, they had to be with the job she was hired to do. After all, Linda and the faculty had Michael Moreno to look after their interests.

When Michael Moreno walked into Catherine's office later that morning, he had to restrain himself from smiling. She was ready for him. No, she looked ready to take on a whole army of negotiators. She had a small conference table set up with stacks of files and reference books, two pots of coffee filled to the brim, and a mountain of pens and legal pads.

She was dressed in a power suit of firehouse red with minimal gold accessories. Her honey-colored hair was swept up in an elegant yet restrained style. Only a touch of makeup, a hint of lipstick. He knew the look well. He'd seen it in the courtroom a hundred times when he confronted a female attorney.

The discreetly feminine attire of yesterday was gone, even though the suit didn't completely hide her delightful figure. This Catherine Walker was ready for battle and his pulse quickened at the thought of matching wits with her.

"Good morning, Michael."

"Catherine."

"I thought you might like a cup of coffee." She motioned toward the coffeepots and the mugs, noticing that he was wearing a white dress shirt tucked into his jeans. Didn't the man ever wear a suit?

"Thank you." He sniffed the aroma appreciatively. "Just the way I like it—strong and black."

As he poured a cup of coffee, he realized something was different about Catherine this morning. And it wasn't just the clothes. She was on to something, and she thought it might make a difference in the power balance of their negotiations.

"Are you settling into Ruth's?" she asked as he seated himself across the table from her.

He nodded.

"Good. Well, why don't we get started, then?"

"Fine with me." Michael's eyes narrowed slightly. Something was definitely up. She was positively smug.

She flipped open a manila folder and handed him a sheet of paper. "I went over the ground rules that you gave me and they seem satisfactory. I'm willing to agree to them today, with one specification that you haven't included. I want it to state that all negotiating sessions will take place here at the college." Catherine was using her administrator's voice. It was low-toned and impartial and, most importantly, it created what she thought was just the right level of authority. She had picked it up from watching female broadcasters on television.

"Did you think I had some other place in mind?" he responded. She was using an official voice, so he matched his tone to hers.

"No, but because you're renting my neighbor's room, thereby creating a situation that could under-mine the professional nature of our relationship, I believe there should be clear boundaries for us."

"That seems to be very important for you," Michael observed.

"It should be for every negotiator." Catherine kept her eyes on the paper in front of her. She was not going to let the conversation take a personal turn.

"Perhaps you're right. Go ahead and add that to the ground rules," Michael agreed. He was an experienced enough negotiator to know when to let the other side take the lead. She must have found something out about his past. Little did she know that people had been trying to use his past against him for the last five years, and it didn't faze him one bit. But he'd let her play her hand out. It could be entertaining.

"I already have. All you need to do is initial the change." Catherine triumphantly handed him a gold pen.

Michael initialed the change. "Nice pen."

"It was a gift from my mother when I took on my job as vice-president," Catherine said absently as she filed the ground rules in her folder. "She was very proud."

So the mother was pushing her, Michael realized thoughtfully. *Not so different from my own parents, always wanting to get me out of the migrant camps.* He forcibly shoved that thought to the back of his mind. He couldn't start feeling sympathy for her, much as he was attracted to the way her soft femininity contrasted with the sharpness of her intelligence. It was a lethal combination for him, and he couldn't afford to be distracted like that. Harmless mind games were one thing. Heart games were another.

"Right, then," Michael said a bit more abruptly than he intended. "Let's get down to work. What I normally like to do is go section by section as we hammer out the contract. The three major areas we have to set out are 'working conditions,' 'grievance procedures,' and 'salary and benefits.' Since working conditions includes everything from the number of classes taught by a faculty member to whatever, we might as well work on that section first. Okay?"

Catherine nodded. She'd been watching the way he used his hands so expressively. The slim gold pen seemed too delicate when held against the dark, roughened skin of his fingers. His strong hand could snap the pen like a match if he didn't hold it carefully.

But he did. Strength and sensitivity. He seemed to possess both qualities, and that was an intriguing combination.

"Catherine? What's the normal class size here?" he was asking.

"Usually about twenty-five for English classes," she responded automatically. *Get with it,* she rebuked herself. *Your job is on the line.* "Other classes can run as high as forty-five or fifty students. We're a small college, so we don't have large lecture classes."

"Even so, it might be a good idea to set a limit."

*True,* Catherine said to herself. She remembered how much more time it took to grade papers in the larger classes. But could she say that? She wasn't the faculty advocate here. She represented management and she had to think from that perspective. Larger classes for full-time teachers meant having to pay for fewer part-time teachers to take up the slack.

"It might not be realistic to suggest class limits," Catherine finally began. "Enrollment in some semesters is higher than others, and the students have to be added to already existing classes."

"You could hire more part-time teachers," he suggested.

"That wouldn't be possible with the annual budget."

"It would be if you made the faculty a priority," Michael responded, keeping his tone low and reasonable.

"The faculty is always a priority here. It's just a matter of what is possible given the dollars that the state allots to us." Catherine couldn't believe that those words were coming out of her mouth. She'd heard President Cramer say them a hundred times, and now she was repeating them like a parrot.

"This is not an issue of money. It's an issue of morale," Michael pressed. "When the faculty knows that they are valued, they work even harder. And that's what you want, isn't it? To have the faculty work to their capacity?"

"Of course," Catherine agreed readily. "But I can't guarantee the kind of money every year that will enable us to live up to this kind of clause. Class size has to remain variable, depending on the enrollment."

After some more discussion, Michael tapped the gold pen on the table. Time to take a pause. They weren't getting anywhere on this issue. "What if we add a proviso that if a class goes beyond a certain number of students, the teacher will have a teaching assistant?"

Catherine watched him closely. *He's cool, that's for sure. And he never boxes himself into a corner.* "That *might* be possible. I'll make a note and write some language to that effect. Of course, we'll have to further define 'teaching assistant' later, whether we're talking about a student assistant or a paraprofessional."

"Of course." Michael observed her carefully write down what they had discussed. This was going to be one long contract. Whatever hope he'd had that Catherine Walker wouldn't know how to do her job as negotiator was blasted. She'd fight for every point, every issue. And why did that prospect delight him? Knowing they'd be closed in this room every day, engaged in a battle of wits?

"Okay." Catherine looked up. "Next point?"

Michael flipped open his legal pad and started through the list of items on working conditions. They argued back and forth on each and every issue, Catherine holding the management line and Michael trying to press for faculty rights. She matched him point for point, never letting up the pressure. And as the morning wore on, instead of wearing down, Michael found himself growing more and more charged from their clashes.

At one point, Catherine leaned forward to drive an issue home and Michael suddenly found his eyes riveted on a tiny mole located on the side of her neck. For some reason, it fascinated him and his mind suddenly went blank. He blinked rapidly, trying to refocus his thoughts. What was the matter with him? He'd never had trouble concentrating before.

Michael jerked to his feet and started to pace across the office. "I need some air," he pronounced as he shoved open the window behind her desk. Michael leaned on the sill and took in a few deep breaths.

"I'll turn the air-conditioning down," Catherine suggested as she walked over to the thermostat. *It is getting warm in here,* she realized. Besides, for the last five minutes, all she'd been able to focus on was a fascinating lock of dark hair that had tumbled over Michael's forehead.

"What do you say about a break?" Catherine offered in a voice that sounded more shaky than she liked. "It's almost one o'clock. And Marilyn should be coming with the sandwiches I ordered this morning. I thought we might eat here and then get back to work."

"Sounds great." Michael rewarded her with an unenthusiastic smile. Then he glanced back out the window at the well-manicured grounds of the college. "Carefully planned. Carefully organized. That's the way you like things, isn't it?"

"It's essential to have things organized. Otherwise you could lose control," Catherine said as she leaned against the edge of her desk, never taking her eyes off his strong profile. The angular planes of his face were saved from severity by the slight upturn to the right side of his mouth. It gave him a rakish appeal— the contrast between strength and humor. And it left Catherine wondering which Michael she liked best: the mocking would-be gas station attendant or the serious union negotiator.

"But you can't always plan your life that way," Michael murmured, still gazing out the window.

"I don't see why not," Catherine said. "Plans give us goals. Goals give us direction. And life needs to have some sort of overall purpose."

Michael's glance swung back to Catherine. That quirk in his mouth was turned up even more to form a lopsided smile that made her heart flip over. "What about the unexpected?"

Catherine crossed her arms around herself defensively. "You can always leave room for the unexpected. Careful planning leaves options, room to maneuver."

"The credo of every management seminar graduate," he spoke in a casual, jesting manner that somehow irritated her. "Don't tell me, you attended all those 'How to Manage' workshops. How to manage people, how to manage your time, how to manage your career."

One glance at her tight lips and he knew the answer.

"And what's wrong with that?"

"Nothing. As long as you realize it's only meant for the work arena. If you try to apply those ideas to your personal life, you're going to miss out on the best part. The spontaneous part. The adventure part."

"I don't think—" She broke off when Michael's sudden movement toward the desk startled her.

Michael thrust both his hands down on the desk and leaned toward her, his face only inches from hers. "What if I suggested that we forget the contract for the rest of the day? We'll go rent a sailboat and sail as far out into the Gulf as we can. What would you say?"

Catherine's throat went dry. "I..."

"How about it, Catherine? Want to do something unplanned? Something just a little wild and crazy?" An excited light glowed in his eyes and it disturbed her more than his actual words. Was he serious? Or was he trying to make her look foolish again, as he had at the gas station?

Her eyes clung to his, trying to read his intention. Was this a new game? If it was, she didn't know the rules. The tension stretched between them and still Catherine found herself unable to speak.

Finally, she cleared her throat lightly and broke the spell. "We'd better finish the work here." She dropped her eyes before his steady gaze.

Michael slowly straightened up, an odd disappointment tugging at his heart. He'd wanted to shake her off her perch of superiority, rattle her cage a little, but he found he was disturbed by the intensity of emotion he'd just felt. If she had given him the slightest sign, they would've been off to find a sailboat. That was how he lived his life now—easygoing and enjoying the moment. But suddenly something more serious seemed at stake and that scared him. The last thing he needed was an emotional entanglement.

"Catherine, I—"

"Lunchtime," Marilyn announced as she pushed open the door to Catherine's office with her foot. She was carrying a tray of finger sandwiches and a small bowl of fruit, which she placed on the conference table. "I believe everything's here that you ordered, Ms. Walker."

"Make sure you put out enough napkins," Catherine reminded her secretary as she deliberately moved away from Michael. That morning it had seemed like a good idea for the two of them to have a working lunch here, but now she wasn't so sure.

Being closed in this room with Michael all day was causing odd things to happen to her perspective. And if she was this off balance after one morning, what would she be like after a week or two in his company? Catherine sent up a silent prayer that the contract would be wrapped up quickly—before Michael Moreno could turn her life upside-down.

"We'll probably work a few more hours, then I'll need you to transcribe some of the points of agreement," Catherine said as she watched her secretary finish setting up the lunch.

"Just give me a buzz when you need me," Marilyn answered.

As she started toward the door, Catherine stopped her. "Leave the door open. It seems a bit stuffy in here. I think we need to have maintenance check the thermostat."

"I'll get right on it." Marilyn carefully left the door half open. "By the way, speaking of maintenance, I have some maintenance requisition forms for you to sign before you leave today."

Catherine nodded and waved her on.

Michael started to say something, but then he stopped as he caught sight of the finger sandwiches. He stared at them for a few moments and then helped himself to small portion. But once he seated himself, he took in the food with anything but casual indifference. Catherine watched in fascination as he devoured the small pile of sandwiches in minutes and then helped himself to a few more.

Feeling her eyes on him, Michael looked up. He offered her a swift smile of apology. "I was trying to be polite, but Catherine, these dainty little sandwiches just don't cut it."

She looked back at him, saying nothing, watching him help himself to a third serving. As he started to pop another sandwich in his mouth, Michael stopped mid bite and sighed loudly. "I can't eat with you staring at me like that. Look, I know this only reinforces the blue-collar image you have of me, but I'm hardly going to pretend that I'm not hungry. The fruit and salad type of lunch just isn't for me. I need real food, and this doesn't even come close. And it's only out of courtesy that I'm leaving some for you," he added as he devoured the last two sandwiches he'd put on his plate.

Catherine's lips suddenly trembled with the need to smile. "I'm sorry, Michael. I didn't do this to starve you. It's just the way that I eat and I assumed you'd want the same. My mistake."

"No problem. That should hold me for a while," he said as he finished the last sandwich. Then he shot a questioning look at her. "But you could make it up by having dinner with me tonight."

Catherine glanced at him skeptically. "Is this another one of these throw caution to the wind propositions?"

"It depends on what you had in mind." A tiny gleam flickered in his eyes. "I was only thinking about dinner."

"How about I make it up to you by ensuring our negotiations go swiftly tomorrow?" she offered, trying to keep her tone of voice disinterested. Actually, the invitation for dinner had caused a sudden racing in her pulse.

He leaned back in his chair, his eyes lazily observing her. "What if I said I'd wear a suit—to dinner?"

"That's not the problem."

"So what is the problem? That you don't want to be seen socially with a guy who wears a T-shirt and jeans?"

"Don't be ridiculous," she responded a shade too quickly.

"I'm only voicing what you don't have the guts to say."

"Or maybe you're misinterpreting me. It just so happens that I have a date tonight. Besides," she paused, bracing herself for his reaction, "that blue-collar act is about as phony as it comes. I happen to know you have a law degree from Harvard." Catherine ended on a flourish, her accusing stare riveted on him.

Michael's expression stilled, and Catherine readied herself for his anger or pained defense. But she was amazed at the calm acceptance that overtook his features. "I was wondering how long it would take before you checked into my background," he said in a reasonable tone. He was still leaning comfortably back in his chair, coffee mug in hand.

"You were?"

"Sure. It's what I'd do in your place. Always know your opposition."

"So you expected it." She tried to keep from appearing disappointed.

He nodded complacently. "It comes with the territory. I've worked on contracts for the last five years and have been the object of the most vicious attacks you could ever imagine. And I've found the best thing to do is always be honest about my background, because the other side will find out anyway and try to use it against me."

Catherine swallowed the large lump that suddenly formed in her throat. That's exactly what she'd been planning to do. She cringed at the obviousness of her behavior.

"So what do you want to know?" he was asking.

"Nothing, really," she wavered. She was too embarassed to press him for more information, much as she wanted to know.

Michael's dark brows rose a fraction. "I do have a law degree from Harvard. Your information was correct there. As for what you call the phony blue-collar act, your information was not so correct. My father was a migrant laborer and I grew up working in the citrus groves here in Florida, so I guess you could say I have a working-class background. However, my mother was a WASP schoolteacher—maybe that makes up for the rest."

"I really didn't mean—"

"To pry? Of course you did. And just to fill in the gaps for you, I did practice the kind of law you'd be proud of—corporate law. Made a lot of money. Had lots of prestige. I had a partnership in Miami and I had a lavish lifestyle. Satisfied?"

"But, why—"

"Why did I give it up?" he finished for her.

"Well, yes," she said frankly.

He took a deep breath. "I could tell you that I wanted a slower-paced life, that I dumped it all to find myself and help humanity. But the truth is, I had no choice. I was forced out of corporate."

Catherine gasped softly.

Michael must have heard her though, because he leaned forward, the right side of his mouth turned up with a wry smile. "You see, I was accused of embezzlement."

# Chapter Four

"I don't believe it," Catherine exclaimed, her face turning pale with astonishment.

"I'll take that as a compliment," Michael said drily. "But it's the truth."

She stared wordlessly at him, her heart pounding with the force of the discovery. It was the last thing she'd expected. He might be undisciplined and careless about his appearance, but she never thought he was dishonest. "Did you go to trial?" she asked slowly.

Michael looked down, studying his folded hands intently. "No. I resigned from my partnership and left Miami and the fast lane far behind. That satisfied my so-called partners, and they didn't press charges. Unfortunately, my fiancée, Felicia, didn't go with me. Strange, but my sudden fall from grace caused her to reconsider our upcoming marriage. I heard she married one of the other partners a year later." He paused and then glanced over at Catherine with a shadow of his lopsided smile. "I went to a monastery in Tibet after that."

"How can you joke about something as serious as this?" Catherine asked incredulously.

Michael's shrug seemed to have a fatalistic air. "I've lived with it for a long time. It was more than five years ago. I laid those ghosts to rest a long time ago."

"But it ruined your life," she blurted, scarcely aware of what she was saying.

"You just don't get it, do you?" he continued in a voice that edged into impatience. "My life wasn't ruined. It changed, that's all—and I can honestly say it was for the better in the long run."

Catherine was more baffled than ever. He'd lost everything and he didn't seem the least bit bitter or unhappy about it. If it had been her, she would have been cursing fate for the rest of her life. To lose all that power and prestige.... Then a sudden thought occurred to her. Perhaps he was guilty of embezzlement. Maybe that's why he was so calm and accepting about the whole thing. He could have ended up in jail if he hadn't resigned his partnership.

"Michael," she began in a hesitant voice.

He raised a hand to rub wearily across his eyes. "I'm not going to defend myself to you or anyone else, Catherine. So if your next question is whether I did it or not, don't bother asking, because I'm not going to answer."

Catherine fell silent. She was swimming in unknown waters and was suddenly out of her depth. The emotions Michael was stirring up were making her uncomfortable. She wanted to believe that he was innocent, but she didn't know if she could trust her own perceptions. Would someone with a lower-class background like his have taken chances, some perhaps even illegal, to further his ambitions? Was that the reason why he couldn't justify himself to her?

When Marilyn appeared at the door once more, Catherine was almost grateful for the distraction. Seeing the familiar, efficient figure in the pink suit seemed like a lifeline of normalcy.

"Bill's on line two," Marilyn informed her. "Do you want me to clear out the lunch things?"

Catherine nodded. She hadn't eaten a thing, but she didn't feel the least bit hungry. As she walked over to her desk, she felt

Michael's dark eyes on her, making her very aware of her every movement. She gave herself a mental shake as she sat down in the leather chair behind her desk. *Get a hold of yourself.* She was letting him turn her into a quivering mass of uncertainties. She was an executive, for goodness' sake. If he was willing to let the good life slip through his fingers, that was his business, but she sure wouldn't have given up what she'd worked so hard for.

Catherine jerked the phone off the receiver with a defiant air. "Bill?" she asked in a cool voice.

"Cathy, just wanted to see if we're still on for dinner tonight," Bill Myers inquired in his usual slow, earnest voice. He'd asked her to check her calendar more than two weeks ago for this dinner date, and then he'd called every three days just to remind her.

"Sure. I'm looking forward to dinner tonight," she emphasized the last two words to make certain Michael Moreno heard her. But as he glance shifted over to him, she noted that he hadn't even heard her. He was conversing with Marilyn, who was smiling in a way that Catherine had never seen before.

"Great. How does the Gardner House sound?" Bill continued.

"The Gardner House?" Catherine repeated even more loudly and emphatically. "Sounds lovely."

As Bill continued to make arrangements for the date, Catherine strained to hear what Michael and Marilyn were saying. Michael was helping Marilyn stack the dishes on the tray and Marilyn was laughing, a light trilling laugh that Catherine had never heard before. Catherine's glance followed the two of them as Michael helped Marilyn carry the tray out of the room and down the hall. She could only catch snatches of conversation, because Bill kept droning on....

"Sorry, what did you say, Bill?" Catherine asked guiltily.

"We could go there if you like," he was saying.

"No, that sounds fine." What had she just agreed to? she thought wildly.

"Which one?"

"I guess...the first one," she struggled for words. For the life of her, she couldn't remember which restaurant he had suggested first.

"The Gardner House?"

"Yes. Yes." She sighed in relief.

"Fine. I'll pick you up at seven."

As Catherine slowly replaced the phone on the receiver, she still wasn't sure what she had agreed to. She'd been so distracted by Michael and his revelation that he was an accused embezzler, she could hardly think straight. And to top it off, he'd actually been flirting with Marilyn—a woman at least ten years his senior and a secretary, for Pete's sake. How could she concentrate on her phone call when the two of them were laughing and joking so loudly that she couldn't even hear what Bill was saying?

"Darn," she muttered to herself.

"Did you say something?" Michael asked as he reentered the room.

"Just talking to myself," Catherine said shortly.

"Did you finish with your call?"

Catherine nodded and smiled sweetly. "It was the man I'm currently dating—Bill Myers. He's the business and finance manager for the college."

"That's nice." Michael seated himself at the conference table again and started sorting through his notes on the contract.

"He wanted to confirm our date for tonight," she pointedly stressed the last few words.

"How thoughtful," he said absently as he scribbled a few lines on his legal pad.

"We've been dating for the last six months," she added.

Michael set the pen down as he let out a long, audible sigh. He focused a sidelong glance on her. "I got the point. You're busy tonight, you're dating someone named Bill, and you want us to keep things on a purely professional level. Message received. So can we get back to work now?"

"Sure," Catherine said in a mollified voice. That was what she wanted, wasn't it? All along she'd been telling him that she didn't want to mix business with her personal life. Then why did she feel so let down?

While Catherine was getting ready for her date with Bill, she simply couldn't shake her feeling of despondency. The afternoon negotiations had gone smoothly. They'd settled quite a few issues with only a minimum of discussion. Michael had been serious to the point of solemnity while negotiating. So what was the problem? They'd covered a lot of ground, and she'd been able to promote the management line through most of it. She had done her job and done it well. Normally that would have had her coming home on a real high. But not tonight.

Maybe it was the weather, Catherine tried to convince herself as she peered out one of the front windows of her bedroom. Even though every window in the room was wide open, not a hint of a breeze stirred the sheer lace curtains draped around them. Summer was just beginning, and the days were growing hotter and wetter—just enough to sap her energy by the end of the day. Soon she'd have to run the air conditioner day and night, just so she could function.

*Yes, it must be the weather that's making me so dispirited,* Catherine assured herself again as she sat down at her dressing table. Dispirited. The word almost made her smile. That's how her mother always said she felt in the Florida summer. A lady never admitted to being depressed, so her mother always said she was dispirited. Never down, depressed, or blue. No, her mother was too refined to use those words.

Catherine swept the side of her hair up in a deep wave and then fastened it with a silver comb. The simple style complemented the classic lines of her knee-length black silk dress. As Catherine started to fasten a long strand of pearls around her neck, she saw her reflection in the mirror and stopped. Didn't she always wear the pearls with this dress? And wasn't the look, well, a little dull?

She dropped the pearls back into the velvet box. As she replaced them in a neat section of her jewelry drawer, she spied a necklace that Ruth had given her years ago. Ruth had cajoled Tom into taking her to Mexico for a vacation and had brought back a turquoise and silver necklace and matching earrings for Catherine. The necklace had always seemed a little flamboyant to her, with its bold squash blossom design and large chunks of turquoise. And the earrings dangled practically to her shoulders. But tonight the necklace seemed just the thing to liven up the black dress.

As she came down the stairs, she heard Bill's knock. Without even glancing at the clock on her fire-place mantle, Catherine knew it was just seven o'clock. Bill was never late, never early. He was always exactly on time. She felt another twinge of despondency at that thought. *What's the matter with me tonight?* she thought. Bill's punctuality had always seemed admirable before tonight. Being on time was a virtue. It meant the man was dependable.

Catherine gave herself a mental shake before she opened the door. She couldn't let any tension between her and Michael at work interfere with her social life. She had to put the emotional turmoil of the day behind her and just enjoy being with Bill. It was true that Bill might not be the most exciting man she'd ever met, but he was smart, dependable, and loyal.

As she resolutely swung open the front door, a tiny protest inside told her those qualities were often used to describe a faithful dog.

"Bill," she said in an overly bright voice. "It's wonderful to see you. Just let me get my purse."

"You look lovely, Cathy," he commented. She saw his glance take in her jewelry with raised eyebrows, but he was too polite to say anything.

As she located her silver evening bag, she asked, "Where are we going for dinner?"

"Cathy, don't you remember what we talked about today?" he responded with a touch of exasperation in his voice.

"I...well, maybe." She waved her hand distractedly as they exited her house and walked toward Bill's car. "You don't know what was going on in my office today when you called. It was total chaos. I could barely concentrate on what you were saying. Sorry."

"That's all right. I've had days like that too," he assured her. "I made reservations at the Gardner House."

"Where? The Gardner House. Great." Catherine couldn't resist a quick glance over at Ruth's house. Her eyes widened as she saw Michael trimming the azalea bushes that stretched across the front of Ruth's house. He was only about halfway finished, yet his shirt was already plastered against his back from the effort of working in the late-day heat. She watched the muscles in his upper arms flex as he worked the trimming shears back and forth across the tops of the overgrown bushes.

He paused and then turned around, meeting her glance squarely. He just stood there, all lean, solid muscle, and Catherine couldn't tear her eyes away.

"Cathy?" Bill was holding the car door open for her.

Catherine blinked twice to clear her vision and smiled shakily. She quickly scrambled into the car and kept her eyes fixed ahead, not daring to look back at Michael.

As Bill backed the car out, he asked, "Who was that? Do you know him?"

"That's Michael Moreno," Catherine said flatly.

"What? He's living next door to you?"

"Let's just get to the restaurant, Bill. I'll tell you the whole story there." She heard the agitation in her own voice and knew Bill probably did too. Hopefully, he would think it was because Michael Moreno upset her with his presence, not because he disturbed her in ways she was only beginning to realize.

Michael watched the tan sedan drive away. He stood motionless for a few moments and then slowly turned back to the azalea bushes. His grip tightened on the trimming shears and he suddenly attacked the bushes with vicious slashes. He hacked up and down at the leaves and branches, the blades of the shears slicing back and forth. His breath started coming in panting gasps, but he kept slamming the shear handles in and out.

"Michael, you don't have to finish trimming today," Ruth said as she poked her head out the front door. "It's too hot to work that hard."

She waved cheerily and then retreated into the house.

Michael halted, taking in deep breaths. What had gotten into him? He had been attacking those poor azaleas as if they were an invading army and his life depended on it. It was as if the floodgates that harnessed his energy had suddenly been thrown open and he couldn't control the surge that had come out. Was it just energy or was it anger? Panting, he dropped down on the front porch step and leaned his arms on the handles of the trimming shears propped up in front of him. It was anger and he had known that kind of anger before.

He was ten years old, working in the fields with his father and the other migrant workers. They'd been toiling in the blazing Florida heat all day with only two water breaks. Michael had watched his father working tirelessly all morning, sweating but never complaining. And then the owner of the citrus processing factory had driven up in his sleek, air-conditioned Cadillac and began inspecting the groves, all the while carefully avoiding any dirt that might soil his impeccable white linen suit. He stopped to talk sharply to Michael's father, never getting too close to the sweat-soaked worker.

Michael felt a surge of anger, picked more oranges with furious precision, and slammed them into the baskets. His father must have sensed Michael's frustration, because he didn't say a word to him for the rest of the day. He just smiled and said he'd worked like ten men that day.

Watching Catherine drive off with Bill had caused a similar surge of burning resentment. And that scared him. He wasn't ten years old. He was a man who'd overcome the poverty of his childhood, driven himself until he'd achieved those trappings of the men who pulled his father's strings. He'd had all the toys, including a beautiful, shallow fiancée who had abandoned him instantly when the rumor of the embezzlement charge reached her ears.

He'd had those empty things and turned his back on them. Now he was using his legal expertise to help the very people who needed him the most and against whom he'd previously turned his back. He traveled to different parts of the state negotiating contracts and settling labor disputes. He never stayed long in one place, and never got emotionally involved. This was the path he'd chosen. So why did the sight of Catherine in the car with that man so enrage him?

She was beautiful, with her honey-blond hair and sky-blue eyes. There was no doubt about that. Being closed up in that conference room with her all day had been a stern exercise in focus and control. But she had more than just looks. Much more. She had a razor-sharp intellect and a subtle sense of humor. She provoked him and attracted him. That was a lethal combination. And one that was dangerous for the success of his assignment as union negotiator on this contract.

"Thought you might like something cool to drink." Ruth was holding a tall glass of iced tea with a mint sprig on the rim. In her other arm was a large tiger-striped tabby.

"Thanks." He gulped down almost half the glass before he stopped to take a breath. He smiled at her sheepishly. "I guess I didn't realize how thirsty I was."

"It's easy to get dehydrated quickly in the Florida heat," Ruth pointed out as she sat down next to him. The tabby curled up contentedly in her lap. "So what do you think of Cathy?"

Michael's grin flashed briefly, white against his olive skin. "You sure get to the point, don't you?" As he eyed Ruth's hot pink tropical print muu-muu and long dangling earrings, he restrained the urge to smile again.

"At my age, there's no time to mess around," Ruth observed. "Besides, people forgive us elderly folks for being blunt. They probably think the areas of the brain that produce tact have burned out with age. But that's okay, because it lets me say whatever I want."

"That's fine with me. I like honesty." He leaned back, sipping the liquid contentedly.

"You still didn't answer my question," Ruth pointed out.

"I didn't say I'd answer. I just said I like honesty," Michael responded.

This time it was Ruth's turn to smile. "Smooth. I like it. It reminds me of my late husband, Tom. He didn't let me get away with anything, and I loved him for it." Her eyes, bright with mirthful remembrance, drifted back to the past.

"You must miss him." Michael detected the glint of sadness in her eyes.

"I do," Ruth was saying. She turned to him, her gray eyes clear and direct once more. "But it's a long time to still be in mourning.

In fact, I'm going to tell you something that Cathy doesn't even know yet. I'm thinking of dating again."

"Anyone I know?"

"That's my secret." Ruth leaned forward, a spark of excitement lighting her face. "At least for now."

Michael nodded in understanding. He knew what it was like to have people poking and prying into one's life. During the embezzlement scandal, nothing was sacred and no part of his life had been spared the intrusive eye of the local press when they were trying to dig into the rumours surrounding him.

"Don't go too long without telling Cathy how you feel," Ruth was saying. "She might end up with that guy."

"How I feel?" Michael asked in a puzzled voice. "I think you've got the wrong idea about us. We're adversaries. Catherine and I are negotiating a contract from opposite sides. I'm not even sure we like each other."

Ruth flapped her hand impatiently. "I may be old, but I'm not stupid. I didn't like Tom when I first met him either, and we were happily married more than twenty-five years."

Michael stared at her, baffled.

"I've got to get ready for my date." Ruth rose up in one fluid motion, shifting the cat onto her shoulder. "Cathy's lost sight of what's really important in life. I blame that fool mother of hers." Ruth shook her head. "But you're the man who can get her back on track. Just don't take too long. I'd hate to see her marry that pie-faced wimp she's been seeing." With a springy bounce, she went back in the house.

Michael's mouth dropped open in amazement. Catherine's mother? What was *that* all about? And who did Ruth think he was? Some kind of knight in shining armor, ready to ride up on his trusty steed and save Catherine from some terrible kind of fate? That only happened in fairy tales.

Michael stood up abruptly and seized the trimming shears once more. Catherine hardly needed rescuing, and he didn't own a horse. Besides, Catherine had chosen to go out with Bill the Worthy and was probably enjoying herself tremendously at some expensive restaurant at this very moment.

Catherine had never been so bored in her entire life. Bill introduced the subject of the college's fiscal budget while they were in the car, then he switched to new accounting software as they entered the restaurant and then continued the theme of the evening with the subject of a new benefits policy. But that's what Bill always talked about on their dates—work. It had never bothered her before. In fact, she had liked talking about work. At least they had that in common. So why was she suddenly so heartily disinterested in what Bill was saying tonight?

"I tell you, Cathy, this new benefits policy is going to save the college a bundle," Bill was pointing out with a self-satisfied air. He took a quick swallow of his wine and then stabbed at a large chunk of his salmon steak and gulped it down. "You know how high the cost of medical care is today, and with our aging faculty, we've got to cut corners before they start moving into their heart attack and stroke years."

"Bill," Catherine exclaimed. "That sounds so heartless."

He shrugged as he dabbed his napkin against the side of his mouth. "It's the way of the world, Cathy. You know that. It all comes down to a matter of dollars and cents."

Catherine was silent. As Bill started to tuck into his salmon steak again with renewed gusto, she found herself losing her own appetite. Her favorite dish of shrimp in garlic sauce sat practically untouched on her plate.

Catherine had thought the atmosphere of the Gardner House would lighten her mood, but now she was feeling even more depressed. It wasn't that the restaurant wasn't romantic, it was, with its intimate little corner tables, antique Victorian lamps, and soft music. All the other couples in there were holding hands and looking deeply and lovingly into each other's eyes. Whereas she and Bill were talking budgets and health policies. That was the depressing note. There was nothing even the least bit flirtatious about their conversation.

"You never said how Moreno came to be staying next door to you," Bill commented in between bites of salmon.

"Oh, Linda Fisher on the faculty told him my neighbor, Ruth, had a room to rent, and he took it." Catherine paused, her face clouding with uneasiness. "To tell you the truth, I'm not really comfortable with the arrangement."

"Why not?" Bill didn't even bother to look up. "With him living so close, you could work on the contract in the evenings too." He almost hummed in satisfaction as he mopped up the last trace of sauce on his plate with a piece of French bread. "That was just deelish," he finally announced, stretching back in his chair to pat his stomach contentedly.

Catherine stared wordlessly across the table at him. Had he always been this insensitive? She tilted her face toward him, resting her arms lightly on the table. "You didn't say how you liked my earrings." She gave a little defiant toss of her head. The earrings tinkled like wind chimes waving in the breeze.

He regarded her critically for a few moments. "They certainly are…different."

"What kind of answer is that? Do you like them or not?" she pressed him, irked by his vague disapproval. *Anything* would be different to a man who always wore a brown suit, brown socks, and brown shoes.

"Of course I do," he said quickly. "I like everything about you, Cathy."

"You do?" A tiny glow began to lighten her mood.

"Do I have to say it?" He reached out and caught her hand in his. "You are so special, different from any other woman that I've known."

"Bill, you've never spoken like this before," Catherine murmured. Why didn't the pressure of his fingers cause the same sparks she'd felt when Michael barely touched her? She immediately squelched the disloyal thought. For goodness' sake, Bill was revealing his heart and she was thinking of another man.

"That doesn't mean I wasn't thinking it," he answered, smiling into her eyes.

Catherine's face brightened at his words. She had been judging Bill too harshly tonight. He might not have the appeal of Michael Moreno, but he was attractive in a clean-cut sort of way, with his carefully cropped sandy hair and regular features. What's more, he came from a good family.

"I mean it when I say special, Cathy," he continued in a sincere voice. "Most women would be bored by business conversation during dinner. But not you. You've got the good sense not to be whining about roses and romance and all that stuff. You're much too levelheaded."

Catherine stiffened in surprise.

"Right after we met, I knew we'd hit if off." Bill squeezed her hands lightly. "We're just so much alike—we're both young, ambitious, and realistic. We share the same goals—work hard, get rich. That's why I enjoy being with you so much. We're so...comfortable together."

"Is that how you really see me?" Catherine asked slowly.

"Of course," he answered without hesitation.

Catherine snatched back her hands as if they were on fire. "I'd like to go home now."

"What?" His eyes reflected his bafflement at her sudden mood change.

"I'd like to go home right now, please." She rubbed a hand across her forehead, shielding her eyes from his questioning glance. "I'm not feeling well all of a sudden." It was true. A cold knot had just formed in her stomach.

"Sure, sure," he answered, motioning to the waiter to bring their check. "I noticed you hardly ate anything."

"Sorry."

Catherine rode home in stony silence. Bill tried to generate conversation a few times, but after receiving Catherine's monosyllables in response, he eventually gave up. She kept her face averted from him the whole time, staring out into the night. When she caught sight of her own reflection in the car window, it seemed a stranger was staring back at her. The up-swept hair was hers, the smooth skin, the widely spaced eyes—but that was just a catalog of features. Nothing in that face told her anything about who the real Catherine Walker was, or how other people saw her. Did everyone see her in the same way as Bill?

When they reached her house, Catherine jumped out of the car. "Please don't bother seeing me to the door. I'll...talk to you tomorrow."

He hesitated. "All right, then. I'll see you—"

Catherine slammed the car door.

As he drove away from the house, Catherine felt a childish urge to stick her tongue out at him. How could he have said those things to her? He made her sound like some kind of emotionless, work-driven robot. Sure, they'd talked about work occasionally on their dates, but that didn't mean she didn't want a real relationship, including roses and romance. He seemed to feel the same emotion for her that he felt for his precious budgets.

Catherine sighed deeply as she stood there in the night. Maybe it was her own fault. She did work long hours. She was the one who always brought up work when she was out with Bill. She had very few interests or hobbies other than work. Heck, how could he see her as anything else but a workaholic?

"Now that's appropriate," a deep, low voice murmured in the distant darkness. "A lady sighing after her boyfriend in the moonlight."

Catherine swiveled around, trying to locate where the voice had come from. As her eyes adjusted to the dim moonlight, she was able to discern the faint outline of Michael Moreno sitting on Ruth's front steps.

"What were you doing? Spying on me?" she demanded.

"If I had I would've been disappointed. There wasn't much to see."

She detected the amused tone in his voice, and it jarred her already-overwrought nerves. "Sorry we didn't put on more of a show for you. I didn't realize you were also a nosy neighbor in addition to your other charming qualities," she grated out before she could stop herself.

She braced herself for his response. But no snappy retort came back at her. She couldn't believe it. She had finally silenced Michael Moreno. Instead of feeling triumphant, though, an odd twinge of disappointment nagged at her. She waited a few more moments in the darkness. Nothing. She turned on her heel and moved toward her front door. Her head was down as she fished through her evening bag for her key. By the time she mounted the front steps, she was muttering to herself, still unable to find the key.

Abruptly, she halted. Michael was blocking her front door. The porch light illuminated his face, revealing an affronted, angry look that was unfamiliar to her. "Look, Miss High and Mighty, don't take your frustrations out on me." His voice was cold.

"I am not frustrated," she countered icily.

"Just because your yuppie boyfriend didn't hang around and kiss you good night, there's no reason to get testy."

Catherine's heart started to hammer in her chest so loudly she was sure Michael could hear it. "I'm not testy, and I don't need a kiss good night," she said shortly. "Now will you please stand aside?"

Michael's gaze burned into her for a few moments. The tension stretched between them like a rubber band ready to snap. Then, to her surprise, he stepped away from her front door. She eyed him warily, but he kept his distance.

Catherine looked down into her purse once more for the key as she moved forward.

"What is it you dislike the most?" he challenged. "Having to work with a guy like me? Or having to live next door to a guy like me?"

"What are you talking about?" she demanded.

"It's so obvious. You don't think I'm up to your social standards, Katie."

"Don't call me—"

"But that's what I'm going to call you—Katie. Just the kind of behavior you'd expect from a blue-collar kind of guy like me, right?"

"So that's what this is all about," she responded, a note of exasperation in her voice. "You think I have some kind of prejudice against you just because you're...well...you're—"

"The son of a migrant worker?" he finished for her.

Catherine was silent. Was he that far off?

"But that isn't the real problem, is it?"

"I... I don't understand."

His eyes darkened with emotion. "The real problem is what are we going to do about this attraction we feel for each other?" Michael put his hand under her chin and turned her face upward. "It doesn't make sense. It's not smart. But there it is. And I'll be darned if I can figure out what to do about it."

Catherine was too astonished to make a sound. Then her emotions surged in sudden waves of tender sympathy as she searched his face. His expression held the dull ache of inner pain—an emotion that was no doubt mirrored in her own face.

Suddenly, he lifted her into the cradle of his arms as she reached out and softly stroked his cheek with the back of her hand. She stood on tiptoe and pressed her lips softly against his.

Michael lost himself in the sensation of kissing her, as she hugged him tightly, her emotions swirling.

## Chapter Five

A car door slammed next door and Michael immediately lifted his head. He felt as if he was swimming in a sea of confused thoughts and feelings and Catherine was the lifeline to his sanity. She was the one reality. He cradled Catherine's head against his shoulder as he tried to catch his breath.

"I... I think that's Ruth coming home from her date," he was finally able to say.

"What?" Catherine asked, trying to comprehend what she was hearing.

Michael pulled back to look deeply into her eyes. He had gone too far. He had let his emotions get out of control, and it had shaken him as much as it had her. The light flirtation of the last two days was turning deadly serious. Catherine was bringing out feelings that he didn't know he was capable of, feelings stronger than he'd ever known before. And he couldn't let it go any further.

"I'm sorry, Catherine," he was saying in a low, vibrant voice. "I... I guess I just got a little wound up today. I didn't mean to let things get so carried away. I know it's no excuse, but I can assure you that I won't let it happen again."

*Why not?* Catherine thought in a daze.

"Catherine?"

The note of apology in his voice snapped her out of her bemused state. Why was *he* apologizing? She was the one who had kissed him. He was probably shocked at her behavior. That's why he was apologizing—to spare her the embarrassment of knowing his true reaction.

"It's all right." She looked down, trying to hide the hurt she knew was revealed in her eyes. "Let's just call it a night, shall we?"

"Catherine, I—"

"I really don't want to talk about it any more tonight, okay?" She started searching desperately in her purse for the front door key again. She had to get inside the house, away from him, before she did something even more foolish—such as throw herself in his arms and burst into tears.

"Okay." The relief was evident in his voice.

Catherine's spirits sank even lower. He obviously thought she was some kind of neurotic workaholic. Where was that blasted key? she almost screamed to herself. She exhaled a shaky breath when she finally found it.

"Good night, then," she murmured as she inserted the key in the lock, opened the front door and then firmly shut it behind her.

As she leaned back against the door, she knew he was still standing there. Why didn't he go? There was nothing left to be said. She'd embarrassed herself enough for one evening.

The shrill ringing of the telephone brought her abruptly back to reality.

She picked up the phone, but, before she was even able to say hello, President Cramer's strident tones came over the lines. "Catherine? I've been calling you all evening."

"I..." She started to justify herself, and then she changed her mind. She didn't owe him an explanation. "I was out with Bill," she stated matter-of-factly.

"Oh? He didn't tell me you were going out," he answered.

"Why should he tell you about our date?" Catherine asked in a curious voice.

"Never mind." He brushed her question aside impatiently. "I asked you to report on the negotiations and I've haven't heard word one from you."

Catherine rolled her eyes toward the ceiling. "This was only our first day on the contract. I assumed you'd want an update at the end of the week when I had—"

"You assumed wrong. Be in my office tomorrow morning at nine o'clock sharp and bring your negotiating notes." He slammed the phone down.

Catherine slammed her phone down in response. "I may work for him, but he doesn't own me," she said aloud. She closed her eyes, suddenly feeling utterly wrung out. She'd been on an emotional roller coaster all evening, and the phone call was the final twist in the track. She didn't know if she was upside-down or inside out.

This couldn't be happening to her. She was the type of woman who planned in the evening what she'd wear to work the next day. She kept a meticulous daily calendar. She never made spur-of-the moment decisions. And here she was making out with a virtual stranger on her front steps and almost telling off her boss over the telephone.

She wasn't the Catherine Walker who had gone to work this morning as she did every morning. Where was that levelheaded, practical executive? Catherine dropped her face into her hands with an anguished sob. All of the control that she had struggled so hard to have over her life was gone. And she was faced with only fear and uncertainty.

Catherine stared at President Cramer across his polished mahogany desk the next morning, carefully noting any changes in his expression as he scanned through her negotiating notes. Though he was leaning back in his chair in a relaxed position, his body language did nothing to convince her to let her guard down for one moment. He was about as harmless as a coiled snake and about as unpredictable in his ability to strike out and put her on the spot.

"You gave in too quickly on providing the option for teaching assistants," he pointed out. "You should've held out for regulating class size according to enrollment."

"I thought of doing that, but giving in on that item allowed me to negotiate committee assignments and office hours in later," Catherine explained.

President Cramer leveled his glance at her over his half reading glasses. "You should've been able to do both. A good negotiator will keep hammering until he gets what he wants."

"I did maintain a management line on all the major items you suggested to me," she continued. "But you didn't highlight this item as one that I needed to go to the wall for." *Keep your cool,* Catherine reminded herself. He had a right to question her.

"Do I have to tell you everything? Outline every strategy?" he responded coldly. "That's your job. If you can't take the initiative on certain items, then maybe I need to have someone else negotiate the contract."

Catherine's hand clenched in her lap. Why was he taking such a personal interest in each and every detail of the contract? That was not like him. And why was she suddenly on trial? Though he'd always been exacting, he'd never been quite *this* critical. "I can finish the contract," she said with quiet firmness. "And I will be more aware of my strategy on every item."

"Good." He removed his reading glasses and tossed them on the desk. His voice softened slightly. "I know I'm being hard on you, Catherine, but I have to keep this college running. If we let the faculty have everything they want, they'll think they can control this college. Besides, they simply don't understand dollars and cents. The college can only provide so much according to our budget."

Catherine smiled and nodded. "I know."

"Let me know by Friday how everything's going." He snapped the file with her notes shut. That was dismissal. Catherine picked up her file and then quickly exited his office.

When she reached her own office, she dropped into her chair and tilted her head back in one fluid motion. It could have been worse, she consoled herself. Aside from the single reprimand, the president seemed fairly satisfied with her work—as satisfied as he could ever be.

This assignment was turning out to be the challenge of her life. Never had she been in a such a difficult position. She'd often heard the expression "between a rock and an hard place," but she'd never really understood it before. Now she did. And both sides were crushing in on her. Not to mention her own feelings for Michael that were exerting their own kind of pressure.

She had awakened this morning with the firm resolution to get control of her growing relationship with Michael. She rehearsed how she would tell him that they had to keep their relationship on a strictly business level. They were here to settle a contract, nothing more. She had her job to consider. It was the most important thing in her life and she couldn't let anyone, even Michael, jeopardize her position at the college.

Besides, nothing could come of a relationship with a man like Michael Moreno. Sure, he was attractive and she found herself drawn to him, but he was the kind of man her mother had warned her about. Face it, he was working class, in spite of his law degree. He was a man who had disdain for professionalism because it had rejected him. Her goals were just too different from his. As a couple, they'd end up like her parents, with her father taking off because he couldn't fit into her mother's world. Both of them hurting each other until they finally had enough and eventually parted ways.

Catherine shook her head. No, she wouldn't end up being hurt like that.

"Good morning," Michael's deep voice interrupted her thoughts.

Catherine snapped back into an upright position, her eyes widening as she took in Michael's appearance. Gone was the easy appeal of his casual shirt and jeans. In its place he wore a beautifully cut gray suit. The jacket fit his wide shoulders smoothly and the pants fell with a perfect crease to his highly polished Italian leather loafers.

His hair was brushed back neatly and had been trimmed in the back so now it barely touched his collar. The whole transformation stunned her. If this was how he had looked in the courtroom during his law practice days in Miami, he must have been a powerful presence.

Michael set an elegant black leather briefcase, complete with cellular phone, on the conference table and pulled out his notes from the previous day. "Shall we get started?" he asked politely.

"Uh...yes, of course," Catherine stammered as she scrambled out of her chair and moved over to the conference table. "There's some coffee over there if you want a cup. Just help yourself. And there's milk and sugar...." She trailed off, knowing she was babbling like an idiot. She was still trying to adjust to the new Michael Moreno who was sitting across the table from her. This man she didn't know. Or maybe she did. Wasn't he the same man she had met the day before yesterday, whom she had kissed last night?

"I like my coffee strong and black," he commented as he poured himself a steaming cup.

"Oh, right. Yes. You said that yesterday."

Michael brought the coffee back to the table and seated himself opposite her. He placed his strong arms on the table and calmly folded his hands in front of him. He looked every inch the powerful attorney in complete command of the situation. "Before we get started, we need to get something straight. First, I apologize for last night. My behavior was inexcusable, and I can assure you it won't happen again. Second, I think we need to maintain the utmost degree of professionalism if we are to bring this contract to a close. Therefore, I suggest we have Marilyn sit in on our sessions and keep a record of all negotiations." His voice was crisp and his face was a blank slate.

Catherine searched vainly for the easygoing, irreverent guy who had flirted with her at the gas station, who had held her so tenderly last night. Instead, a gray-suited, cold-eyed stranger sat across from her. But that's what she had wanted, wasn't it? To keep the negotiations on a purely business level? She took a deep, steadying breath. "I accept your apology. We both got a little carried away last night and I think the whole incident is best forgotten. As to your suggestion of a third party on these negotiations, I think that might be...helpful."

"Good."

"I'll buzz Marilyn, then." Catherine pressed the intercom to signal to her secretary that she was needed. While they waited, Michael began arranging his materials on the conference table.

"I brought the state board of education rule book in case any questions come up today," he commented briefly as he flipped through his legal pad. "And I have some sample contracts from other colleges that you might want to scan."

"I've previewed other contracts, but thank you anyway." Catherine's tone was as formal and distant as his and, for some reason, it disheartened her rather than reassured her. Now Michael was like every other executive she'd ever met. The same clothes, the same hair, the same voice. *That's what professionalism is all about, isn't it?* she asked herself.

When Marilyn entered the room with her tape recorder and steno pad, Michael turned to Catherine, surveying her impassively. "Where did we leave off yesterday?" Catherine sighed as she opened the file with her notes. "We were up to committee assignments and office hours."

"Okay, let's get to it," Michael said without any degree of enthusiasm.

Michael was as good as his word. After that day the negotiations went smoothly, with none of the flirtatious, charged exchanges that had characterized their first session together. Catherine realized her secretary's presence had something to do with that. Having a third party there with a tape recorder certainly helped to keep a lid on their emotions. Not that they didn't argue about certain issues—but when they disagreed, they were more like two lawyers squaring off against each other in the courtroom, using only the force of their reason and argument to convince the other person.

Even worse, Catherine rarely saw Michael outside of the actual negotiating sessions. Each day he took a lunch hour alone and, after the sessions were over each day, he disappeared. Catherine found herself thinking up a lot of excuses to work in her yard every evening. She had planted just about every type of flower and bush that was native to Florida, but she still didn't see him so much as snip one branch of Ruth's azaleas. Catherine had even gone so far as to make a few evening trips over to Ruth's car to pick up some oranges, but each time Michael was nowhere to be seen. Ruth said nothing, but Catherine sensed she knew the real reason behind Catherine's sudden desire for oranges.

The upshot was, as the days passed, Catherine realized that the contract was progressing nicely, she was maintaining a management line as much as possible, and the president was satisfied with her work. She should have been delighted. Never had she been flying on such a professional high. Everything was proceeding smoothly, just the way she had hoped. Wasn't it?

"It looks like we'll have the working conditions section finished by the end of the day," Michael said at the end of the second week. He locked his hands behind his head and leaned back comfortably in his chair. "If we can keep up this pace, we have the whole contract finished in a couple of weeks."

"So soon?" A tiny alarm went off in Catherine's head. Would she ever see him again?

Michael nodded with a look of satisfaction. "I think so. Things may even move more quickly after we finish this section. This is the tough one. It has so many nitpicking details. I want to thank you for carefully keeping track of them."

"Well, I—" Catherine broke off when she realized Michael was thanking Marilyn, and what was worse, her secretary appeared to be blushing. A woman of her age. Catherine suddenly wondered if there was anything going on between the two of them. She immediately squelched the thought. That was absurd.

"Thanks, Michael," Marilyn was saying as she clicked the tape recorder off. "But you and Ms. Walker make my job so easy, it hardly seems like work."

Michael flashed Marilyn one of his lopsided smiles, which Catherine had been longing to see for the last seven days. To her secretary, of all people.

"Marilyn?" Catherine's brows rose deliberately to remind her secretary of something she had to see to.

Marilyn nodded and then quickly exited the room.

"In light of our success over the last week, I've got a little surprise for you," Catherine said as she eagerly started clearing their materials off the conference table.

"What would really surprise me is to see you thank a subordinate someday," Michael murmured, half to himself.

"What?" Catherine was busily stacking files.

"Nothing." He repressed a sigh as he looked out the window. The Florida sky was the color of a blue topaz, sharp and clear, without a single cloud on the horizon. It was a day meant for sailing. Drifting on the water and dreaming lazily. But not with Catherine. Her life hummed only to the tune of work. And she expected him to sing the same song.

It had been difficult these last two weeks to act that way, but he had done it. He'd conformed to exactly what she expected. He pretended to be interested only in work. He treated her as a colleague, as if he were not aware of her warmth and loveliness just across the table from him. Never had he been able to negotiate a contract so quickly and never had he been so frustrated. But that was how Catherine wanted it. Completely professional. She might have given in to her romantic impulses that night on her porch, but she could never love a man who wasn't ambitiously climbing the corporate ladder. Just like Felicia. *She* had loved him only as long as he was a successful and powerful attorney. Once that dissolved, so did her love for him.

But he hadn't counted on his feelings for Catherine being so strong. When Felicia left him, he'd almost been relieved to leave her behind with all the other shallow trappings of his former life, but seeing Catherine just drive off with Bill that night stunned him with the intense jealousy that ripped through him. He couldn't let himself be that vulnerable ever again.

"So what do you think?" Catherine was saying. She swept her hand across the table in a dramatic gesture. Michael followed the movement and was momentarily taken aback. There was a footlong, three-layer sub sandwich, potato salad, and chips.

"A man's lunch," Catherine pronounced.

"I'd say that would fill ten men." A flash of delight crossed his face.

"Sorry, it's only nonalcoholic beer," she apologized as she handed him a large glass with liquid foaming at the rim.

"It'll do," He took the glass from her, their fingertips barely brushing. It was the first physical contact they'd had since that night on her porch, and Michael frowned slightly at the tiny current he felt from her fingertips.

"Is this okay?" Catherine asked quickly, noting his frown.

"Great." He helped himself to a large section of the sub sandwich and a generous portion of potato salad. "More than great. Primo."

Catherine helped herself to a small piece of the sandwich and a few chips. She slid into the chair next to Michael's and propped her feet up on the chair across from her. Michael's gaze slid down the slim length of her legs, his eyes lingering on her delicately curved ankles.

He tilted his head back and his glance came back to her face. "We're not on opposite sides of the table for once."

"Food is the great equalizer." Catherine held up her part of the sandwich and contemplated it with mock seriousness. "Besides, I think we've earned a small respite."

"Are you sure? We are, after all, adversaries," Michael said, a smile tugging at his mouth.

Catherine regarded him speculatively. "Maybe not adversaries. More like advocates—only for opposite sides."

Michael mulled that over for a few moments while he savored his sandwich. "Not necessarily hostile, then."

"We could be downright amicable."

He gave a short bark of laughter. "Ms. Walker, are you trying to flirt with me?"

Catherine grinned at him. "I wouldn't think of it, Mr. Moreno."

Michael turned his attention back to his sandwich, shaken by the power of her smile to cause a leap in her pulse rate. "I'm glad to hear it. I wouldn't want your boss to think you were fraternizing with the enemy."

Catherine instantly sobered. That's exactly how President Cramer would interpret her behavior. All at once, her office picnic idea seemed inappropriate. She placed the uneaten portion of her sandwich back on her plate and then dabbed at her mouth with her napkin. She rose from the conference table and moved over to her desk. Lightly, she ran her hand across the shiny cherry wood veneer top. "I know you probably think I'm obsessed with work." Her voice reached out to him, soft and uncertain for the first time.

"I–"

Catherine silenced him with a wave of her hand. "You don't need to say it. And you'd be right. I guess I am preoccupied with my job." She turned to face him as she leaned against the desk, her arms folded across her chest defensively. "It's just that...work has always been the one stable thing in my life. No matter how crazy everything gets, I always have my work. It's constant, solid, and dependable."

"And people aren't like that," Michael finished her point softly.

"Right." She shook her head. "How well I know that. My father was one of those people who couldn't decide what he wanted to do. He drifted from job to job. My mother covered up for him, but everyone knew he couldn't stick with anything. Eventually he just left us too."

"Why?"

Her face settled into a brittle smile. "I don't know why. What does it matter? He died five years ago on the other side of the country, chasing some new dream around California, no doubt."

"There's nothing wrong with having a dream." Michael wanted to hold her tightly, banish those shadows that lurked in the blue depths of her eyes. But those were her ghosts. He couldn't make them go away for her. "Unless—"

"Unless it gets mixed up in other people's reality," Catherine said with some asperity. Then she tossed her head back defiantly. "Nobody ever got anywhere in this world except with hard work. And what's wrong with that? A little ambition will bring you a little success. A lot of ambition will bring you a lot of success."

"That's what I used to tell myself." Michael's voice was smooth but insistent. "I thought I was on the road to success. But I wasn't. It was an empty highway to nowhere."

Catherine straightened and walked forward, stopping in front of Michael. "I don't think you really believe that. You were forced to turn your back on the good life. Look how well we've worked together in the last two weeks. You've got all the right moves to be successful in a big way again. You could have it all again if you wanted to."

He wondered if that meant he could have her too. Would he have to sell his soul again to win her? He started to stretch his hand out toward her, and then he pulled it back. No, the stakes were too high. He couldn't live that kind of life again, not even for her.

Michael shook his head decisively and then turned back to the conference table. "Perhaps we'd better try to finish this section before we call it a day."

Catherine wavered, trying to comprehend his sudden mood shift. She'd just been attempting to reassure him that he could jumpstart his career again if he wanted to. He may have thought the road he'd been on had led nowhere, but was the one he was on now any better? He had neither position nor respect. He was wasting his legal background on this union contract work.

The ring of Michael's cellular phone in his briefcase cut into her thoughts.

"Moreno here," he said curtly.

As his expression grew guarded, Catherine suspected the call must be from the union headquarters in Tallahassee. "I need to check with Marilyn for a few moments." She made a slight gesture toward the door and then stepped out of the room.

"Okay, go ahead, Harry. I'm alone now," Michael urged.

"Where are you in the negotiations?"

"Almost finished with working conditions. We'll probably start on grievance policy on Monday—and then salary and benefits."

"Good. Then you can request the budget without sounding like you're jumping the gun."

"What's going on?" Michael asked, growing concerned. Harry Shelton was the general counsel for the union, and when he called, there was trouble brewing.

"Nothing I can put my finger on. Just rumors." He sounded hesitant.

"Come on, Harry," Michael prompted.

"Okay, here's the deal," he continued matter-of-factly. "There have been some rumors about mismanagement of funds at the college. We're going to do a little investigating from our end, and you need to go over that budget with a fine-toothed comb at your end."

"What do you mean, mismanagement? Are there missing monies? Errors in the budget? What are you talking about?" he pressed for more information.

"I can't say right now." Harry's tone was evasive. "I do know that whatever's going on, all the top administrators are probably in on it."

Michael's breath caught in his lungs. "All of them?" he managed to get out.

"I'm afraid so. Sniff around. Find out what you can. Maybe this woman you're negotiating with—"

"Catherine Walker."

"Right. Maybe she'll get nervous and give you some information. After all, she's the new girl on the block, and if the administration goes down, she'll be the one to take the fall whether she's part of it or not."

"I'm supposed to negotiate with her. Not investigate her," Michael protested.

"So what?" Harry countered. "If she's been doing illegal stuff, she deserves it. If not, then she's got nothing to worry about. At any rate, I'll check with you early next week."

As he clicked the phone off, Michael stared ahead of him in stunned disbelief. Catherine couldn't be involved in anything illegal, could she?

# Chapter Six

"So, where were we?" Catherine asked as she came breezing back into the room.

Michael stared at her blindly. He took in her light gray suit, beige blouse, and carefully styled hair that fell to her shoulders in a honey-colored fall. There was both delicacy and strength in her face. But was there dishonesty?

"Is something wrong? Did you get bad news?" she asked in sudden alarm. He was looking at her so strangely.

Michael blinked twice. "No, not at all. I...uh...was thinking about all the work that we have to finish this afternoon."

Catherine slid into the chair next to him. "Look, it's Friday. We've been working like dogs on this contract all week and we need a break."

"Why, Ms. Walker, are you actually suggesting that we take off early?" He leaned close and whispered the last words to her in a dramatic voice.

She leaned forward until her face was only inches from his. "Yes, I am," she whispered in an equally dramatic voice.

"I'm shocked to my very soul." Michael drew back and placed a hand over his heart.

"Hey, you're the one who's always telling me I need to loosen up, so I'm just taking your advice," Catherine said in mock protest.

"Besides, I just found out that Marilyn has to knock off early because one of her kids is sick."

"Ah," Michael said knowingly.

"I would've suggested it anyway," she defended herself.

"Right."

"To tell you the truth, I'm a little tired. So why don't we have another cup of coffee and wrap it up?" she suggested as she refilled their mugs. But it wasn't the work that had suddenly drained her. It was the emotional exchange that she'd just had with Michael. Thinking about her father always upset her, and actually talking about him with Michael had practically wrung her out. "How about it?" She held out a mug to him as if it were a container of appeasement.

He hesitated, then took it from her. "You convinced me."

"Good." Catherine glanced through her notes, still on the table. "We can finish up this last section on working conditions on Monday. Then we can attack the grievance procedure. I've read some models on grievances and picked out a couple that I like." She handed him two files. "Maybe you could look them over this weekend and then we can get a jump start on them early in the week."

"Organized and efficient—as always."

Catherine set her chin in a stubborn line. "I'm doing my job, that's all."

"I meant it as a compliment," Michael said gently. Was she as vulnerable as she appeared to be at that moment? Or was it all part of her act? He had to know one way or the other. It could be that she was involved in some kind of conspiracy. "By the way, I'd like to have a copy of the budget so I can get ready for the salary and benefits section."

"No problem."

He observed her closely as she scribbled a note to herself. Her reaction wasn't any different from any number of times over the last two weeks when he'd requested information from her. But she could be faking it.

"I'll talk to Bill about getting you a copy. Last year's and this year's?" she inquired.

He nodded, not trusting himself to speak. The mention of Bill's name caused him to clench his jaw.

"Anything else?" Catherine looked up and saw the tense set of his jaw. She quickly looked down as though to check her notes, but all the while her heart was pounding with delight. He wasn't as immune to her as he'd pretended to be the last two weeks.

He looked over his schedule book for a few moments. "Not really. Oh, I almost forgot. I'm supposed to pick you up at seven tonight."

"What?"

"It says right here." He held up the daytimer and pointed at the date. "Yes, here it is. Friday: Pick up Catherine at seven."

A smile played at the corner of her lips. "I don't recall making that date."

"Daytimers don't lie. You must have forgotten." His eyes clung to hers, waiting for her reaction. He tried to tell himself that he was anxious for her answer because he had to get information about any fund mismanagement. But, deep inside, he knew that wasn't true. He simply wanted to be with her. It had been pure hell to have her so close yet so far out of his reach the last few weeks.

"And just exactly what did I agree to do tonight?" she asked.

"That's for me to know and you to find out."

"Seriously. Where are we going?"

"Seriously." He took her hand, never moving his eyes away from hers. He lowered his voice, being purposefully mysterious. "I can't tell you."

She snatched her hand back. "Why not?"

"It's a surprise."

"But what will I wear? I need to know."

"Why?"

"I just do."

He stood up and pushed his hands deep into his pockets. "Can't you be spontaneous?"

Catherine opened her mouth to respond and then stopped. No, she couldn't. He was right. She couldn't remember when she'd done *anything* on the spur of the moment. Except when she'd kissed him on her front porch. A faint flush spread across her cheeks at the memory.

A slow, easy smile came over his face as he realized what she was thinking. He put his hand under her chin and turned her face up to his. "Now *that* was spontaneity."

*"That* was reckless." She had to fight the urge to turn her cheek and rub it against his hand.

"Who cares? I don't regret it. Do you?" he asked in a soft voice.

Someone cleared his throat loudly. Michael immediately stepped back. Catherine saw, to her horror, that Bill Myers was standing in the doorway.

"Bill, I was just going to call you," Catherine said in a voice that she hoped sounded more composed than she actually felt.

"Yes, I can see that." Bill's voice was heavy with sarcasm.

"Negotiating a contract is delicate work, Bill," Michael stressed his name with a cold edge of irony. "It requires the personal touch."

"Just what are you getting at, Moreno?" Bill demanded.

"Nothing," Catherine interrupted as she moved to stand between the two men. "Michael was joking, that's all."

For an instant, Michael's eyes narrowed ominously as he looked over her head at Bill. Then as she turned around, he saw her eyes.

They were pools of appeal. "Sorry. I guess not everyone appreciates my sense of humor," he said in a lighter tone. "Ms. Walker is practically a saint to put up with me." Michael realized that antagonizing Bill Myers would only make it hard for Catherine and, even if she was involved in some kind of conspiracy with that jerk, Michael couldn't do that to her.

Catherine's laugh had a false ring even to her own ears. "I don't think I'm quite ready for sainthood."

Bill's glance moved from Michael to Catherine and then back again. Apparently satisfied, he visibly relaxed. "Sorry, Moreno. I guess I don't understand that type of humor. I'm more of a dollars and cents man."

"Not much sense at all," Michael murmured to himself.

"What?" Bill's brows rose questioningly.

"Nothing."

Catherine coughed nervously. "I don't think we have anything else to discuss today, Mr. Moreno, do we?" She gave a silent prayer that he would leave without making any more pointed comments to Bill. The last few minutes had been like walking through a mine field for her, not knowing what Michael would say next. However much her personal relationship with Bill had deteriorated, she had to maintain his professional goodwill.

"I don't think so, Ms. Walker." He winked at her as he left the office.

Catherine looked down, trying to suppress a smile.

"Cathy, I don't like that man's attitude," Bill commented tersely. "I can see where you might have trouble working with him. He doesn't seem to take any of this seriously."

*No, he just doesn't take you seriously,* Catherine inwardly corrected him. "I haven't had trouble working with him, Bill. In fact, negotiations have been proceeding smoothly." She started to gather up her notes and files that were spread across the conference table.

"Cathy, I've been leaving you messages all week and you haven't returned a single one." He lowered his voice, his eyes darting out the doorway and then back to Catherine. "What gives?"

"I've been busy with this contract," she replied in a crisp, impersonal tone. "If you need an appointment, I'm sure Marilyn can see to it."

He gave a snort of exasperation. "I'm not talking work, Cathy."

"Well, that's a switch," she said sarcastically.

"Is that the problem?" he asked, an impatient edge to his voice. He quickly moved around the table and startled Catherine by grasping her shoulders. "Ever since that dinner, you've been acting distant. I'm sorry I'm not romantic enough for you, but you never acted like that mattered before."

Her gaze faltered before his questioning one. "Well, it does."

"Just because I don't wear my heart on my sleeve doesn't mean I don't feel anything for you," he was saying. "And if you want more romance, I can supply that."

"It's not a commodity, Bill," Catherine said quietly.

The room fell silent for a few moments. Bill dropped his hands and Catherine resumed tidying up her files.

"Oh, I almost forgot." She stacked the files on her desk. "Mr. Moreno requested a copy of the budget for last year and this year."

Bill bristled visibly. "Why would he need that?"

Catherine released a long sigh of frustration. "Because that section of the contract will be coming up soon and we'll have to start talking about faculty raises."

He still hesitated. "I'm not sure that he's entitled to see the budget from last year. The only one that would pertain to this contract is this year's. And I don't see why we have to give him a copy of that budget either."

"Bill, why are you being so stubborn about this?" she asked in puzzlement. "It seems a simple enough request. Besides, if we don't provide it for him, he can legally demand a copy because it's a matter of public record."

Bill frowned. "I hope you didn't tell him that."

"I think he probably knows," she said dryly.

"Whose side on you on, anyway?" Bill accused her.

Catherine studied him and said nothing. Even when he was angry, his features remained bland.

"Well?" he persisted in a nasty tone.

"I'm not going to dignify that question with an answer, Bill. I think you know me well enough by now to understand where my loyalties lie. And if you don't, that's just too bad." Catherine slammed the rest of the files down on her desk.

Bill looked contrite. "I didn't mean to insult you, but this whole budget thing just unsettled me."

Catherine bit her lip to refrain from saying anything insulting. The budget was Bill's territory and it was natural that he should feel threatened, but not to the extent of this type of paranoia.

"I'll have copies for you on Monday." His tone was apologetic. Then he added on an even more persuasive note, "So where are we going tonight?"

Catherine leaned her elbow on the stack of files and regarded him speculatively. "Tonight?"

"It's the third Friday of the month," he reminded her. "We have a standing date every third Friday."

Catherine closed her eyes in chagrin. Had she been living that kind of structured life all this time? Was she so inflexible that dates were penciled in as though they were any other appointment on her calendar? "I'm afraid I'm going to have to cancel our regularly scheduled date for tonight," she informed him with quiet emphasis.

Bill's brows reached for the ceiling in shock. "But we've gone out every third Friday for the last six months," he protested.

"I know. That's the problem."

He threw up his hands in exasperation. "I don't understand you anymore, Cathy. You're not the same woman I started dating six months ago."

"Maybe not. Maybe I don't want to be."

"This is ridiculous talk," he muttered. "I'll be at our usual restaurant tonight, and if you're not there, you can just forget about us getting together any other night." He marched out of the office and Catherine heard a door slam down the hall.

A smile trembled over her lips. It spread across her face and, suddenly, she couldn't help herself as she burst out laughing. It was a deep, full-bodied laugh, coming from deep within her, lasting a several minutes until she was practically weak. When it had passed, she took in a deep, cleansing breath and smoothed down her hair. She couldn't remember when she had laughed that hard and long, and she left the office with a tiny smile still curving her mouth.

It was ten minutes after seven when Catherine heard her doorbell ring. She almost jumped in excitement. Since Michael hadn't told her where they were going, she'd debated for more than an hour about what to wear. She'd tried on six different outfits, but each one seemed too formal or too casual for whatever lay ahead this evening. Finally, she had decided on a navy sleeveless sweater and soft yellow linen walking shorts. She then fastened an abstract print silk scarf in blue and yellow around her waist as a belt.

As she checked in the mirror one more time, she took in the whole picture. Casually elegant. Her hair fell to her shoulders, softly curving under at the ends, and her makeup was only a hint of peach color on her eyes and lips.

The doorbell rang again.

*This is silly to keep standing here, staring at myself,* Catherine thought. But she looked different tonight and it wasn't the clothes. That perpetual strain she had started to notice on her face was gone. Her mouth didn't have that slight downward turn and the tiny frown line between her eyebrows had disappeared. She felt positively lighthearted.

Humming to herself as she skipped down the stairs, she didn't pause to think why she felt almost absurdly happy. It was enough simply to feel it. She hadn't felt like this in a long time. Actually, she couldn't remember when she'd ever felt this way.

She threw open the door just as Michael was extending his finger out to press the doorbell again. "I thought you might be having some trouble with your doorbell," he commented as he took in her appearance, from her shining hair to her slim legs. How could she look so fresh and pretty after a difficult day in the office?

Catherine's face fell as she took in Michael's gray T-shirt and sweat pants. "Am I overdressed?"

"Not for what you're going to be doing," he said enigmatically.

"What *am* I going to be doing?" she asked with a small twinge of alarm.

"You'll see."

"But, Michael—"

"Let's live a little. Come on." He put an arm around her waist and tried to propel her out of the house as Catherine held on to the doorknob. "Spontaneity, remember?"

The mischievous glint in his eyes was urging her to let go. And not just of the doorknob. A familiar shiver of awareness rippled through her at the pressure of his fingers against her waist. His closeness was causing her senses to go haywire and she was ready to go anywhere he would take her. "Okay," she said breathlessly.

"Good." He planted a light kiss on top of her nose. "Let's get going."

Catherine blinked at the unexpected intimacy of the kiss, but he obviously thought nothing of it because he was already halfway to his car.

"Wait a minute." Catherine stopped short as she caught sight of the gleaming pink Cadillac. "That's Ruth's car. How—? What—? It looks fantastic." She peered inside but didn't see even a single orange.

"It's a beauty, isn't it?" He ran a hand across the hood. "Ruth said she and her new gentleman friend needed transportation, so I suggested that we bring this old dinosaur out of retirement. I cleaned it up, overhauled the engine, and polished it within an inch of its life."

"It's gorgeous," she exclaimed as she took in the shining chrome bumpers and gleaming tail fins rising up in back like giant wings.

"May I?" He held the door open for her and she climbed into the cavernous interior.

"Michael, that was a wonderful thing to do for Ruth," she pointed out as he slid in behind the steering wheel. She spoke in an odd, gentle tone. "For me too. This car was made the year I was born. Ruth used to tell me how she and her husband drove it down here when they first moved to Florida."

Michael made a dismissive gesture with his hands. "I was motivated by purely selfish reasons, Katie." He looked over at her, his brows arched suggestively. "I've always wanted to drive a blond around town in a pink Cadillac." He shifted the car into gear and accelerated slowly down the palm-lined street that ran through the center of the residential district.

Catherine's laughter trilled in silvery tones through the car. She pressed the button to roll the window down and then turned her face toward the breeze that whipped through her hair. This was absurd—riding in this thoroughly ludicrous-looking car. She should feel foolish, she should insist he stop the car and get out as fast as she could, she should run to the next town to escape this crazy feeling she had when she was with him.

Instead, she reached out and covered his hand with hers.

## Chapter Seven

"Why are we stopping here?" Catherine asked in puzzlement as Michael turned the car into the gravel parking lot next to the local baseball field.

"Haven't you ever been to a baseball game?" he inquired.

"As a matter of fact, no." Catherine's tone suggested that she didn't particularly want to see one this evening.

Michael grinned. "Then tonight's your lucky night. You're about to be initiated into the mysteries of Little League baseball—America's greatest summer pastime."

"Are you sure you don't want to go somewhere else for a quiet dinner? Take a stroll down by the marina? A drive out to the beach?" Her brain searched frantically for alternatives. It wasn't that she didn't like baseball. It just seemed like such a noisy display of emotion and energy, not to mention all the dust and dirt.

"Relax, Catherine. I promise you'll have a good time," Michael reassured her.

Catherine's nod was doubtful.

As they approached the playing field, Catherine's eyes widened. There were hundreds of people there, all talking and clamoring with excitement at the prospect of their sons and friends taking part in Little League. She must have driven past this park a hundred times on her way to and from work, but she'd never noticed any of the baseball games going on.

"I had no idea—" Catherine began, but was cut off as a group of young boys swarmed around Michael and her.

"Mike, where have you been?" they all said in unison.

"I had to pick up a friend. This is Ms. Walker." He gestured toward Catherine, who smiled uncertainly at the cluster of eager faces turned up toward her.

"Hi," she said with a little wave of her hand.

"Are you going to watch the game?" asked one red-haired boy who looked vaguely familiar.

"Yes...yes, I am." She cleared her throat awkwardly and glanced at Michael. There was an unholy glint in his eyes. He was relishing her discomfort. So what if she was a little ill at ease around children? It didn't mean she didn't like children. She just didn't have many opportunities to be around Little Leaguers. Keenly aware of Michael's scrutiny, she took a deep breath and flashed the boys an open, friendly smile. "And I'm really looking forward to seeing you win tonight."

They rewarded her with shouts of approval. "She's all right, coach," the small chorus chanted.

"Coach?" Catherine shot a quick glance at Michael.

"Didn't I tell you?" he replied evenly. "I'll be coaching the game and you'll be part of the audience."

"But, Michael—"

He gave a helpless little shrug as the group of boys drew him off toward the baseball diamond. "I'll catch you later," his voice rose above the clamoring exclamations of the boys, each vying for his attention.

Catherine watched in dismay as Michael moved farther away from her. So this is where he'd been every night when she'd been practically denuding her entire yard in an effort to get his attention.

If only she'd known. She could have avoided the hot, sweaty labor *and* saved her nails.

Catherine smiled ruefully. Michael Moreno was an ever-changing mystery to her. She never knew what he was going to do from one minute to the next, but he could always be counted on to do the unexpected. What she thought was going to be a date turned out to be an evening of Little League. Talk about unanticipated. But it was still better than being bored to death all night by Bill, she reminded herself.

As Catherine's glance swept over the crowd that was practically roaring in anticipation of the beginning of the game, she started to respond to the restless energy in the atmosphere. It was a cloudless, warm evening—the sun had mellowed into a golden ball. But the park was crackling with excitement. And all because of a bunch of kids playing baseball, she thought in amazement.

"Cathy!" a voice shouted above the din.

Catherine looked up into the bleachers and saw a hand waving wildly. It was Linda Fisher.

"Linda, what are *you* doing here?" Catherine asked her friend breathlessly when she'd completed her climb to the top of the stands where Linda was seated.

"I was about to ask you the same question."

"Michael asked me." As Linda's brows began to rise in speculation, Catherine continued, "Just as a friend, that's all. He thought I might like to—"

"To watch a Little League game?" Linda finished on a doubtful note. "And in that outfit?"

"I *am* wearing shorts," she protested. But it was a far cry from what Linda wore—jeans and the bright fuschia T-shirt with HOT MAMA scrawled across the front.

"Always the fashion plate," Linda gently ribbed her.

"To tell you the truth, I didn't really know we were coming here tonight," Catherine confessed.

"Oh? Did you have something else in mind with the handsome and very virile Mr. Moreno?" Linda asked archly.

"Of course not," she immediately denied the implication. But was that the truth? Hadn't she daydreamed about him all afternoon? She glanced over at Linda and caught the wicked sparkle in her friend's green eyes. "Well...maybe I wasn't exactly expecting a ball game," Catherine confessed with a guilty smile.

"I don't see why not. I can't imagine anything more romantic," Linda pointed out in a mock serious voice.

Catherine gave a short laugh. "So why are you here, Linda?"

"My son, Mark, is in Little League." She pointed at the boy standing next to Michael. "He's the red-haired menace with freckles who you were just talking to."

Catherine's jaw dropped slightly in surprise. "I didn't know. I mean, I knew Mark was involved in sports after school, but you never told me he did Little League. And I haven't seen him in so long."

"I guess it never came up." Linda shrugged.

A stab of guilt shot through Catherine. It hadn't come up because she'd been so work-obsessed that she never encouraged her friend to talk about her son. All this time the two of them had been friends, Catherine could hardly recall talking about really personal subjects that mattered.

Linda cast an understanding glance at Catherine. "Don't feel bad. I don't expect my single friends to be that interested in my son's activities. It's different if you have kids." She turned back to the baseball field. "It's all just a matter or priorities."

*Priorities. I've had only one: work.* Catherine's eyes swept over the other parents in the crowd. They were so thrilled to see their kids play Little League. They probably all had jobs like Linda, but they still found time to spend with their children on things that mattered most to them. They had their priorities where they counted—with the people they loved most. But then again, they probably just had jobs. She had a career.

And where did Michael fit into her life? Was he becoming a priority for her?

"Didn't you know that Michael was coaching?" Linda asked.

Catherine shook her head. She could see Michael in a huddle with the boys on his team. They were looking up at him raptly, hanging on his every word. Michael playfully rubbed the hair of one of the boys, who then pretended to punch him in the stomach. The whole group of boys then laughed.

"When I heard he'd played some minor league baseball, I asked him if he would give our boys a few pointers. I never dreamed he would take them on as a temporary coach. He's so good with the boys," Linda enthused.

*Minor league baseball? What other tricks did Michael have in his bag?* Catherine speculated.

"Mark just loves him," Linda was saying. "A boy his age needs a male role model with his father gone so much." She ended on a sigh.

"You miss Joel a lot, don't you?"

"Miss him?" Linda's mouth turned up into a funny little smile. "So much, it's hard to believe that I could feel that way about anybody."

"But you both knew he'd be gone a lot because of his job," Catherine reminded her gently.

"Yes, but nothing prepares you for the way you feel after you're married to a man. After you have a child together...." Her voice trailed off.

Catherine uncharacteristically slid an arm around her friend's shoulders. Linda leaned her head down for a few moments and then blinked away the tears that started to spill down her cheeks. "I don't know what's the matter with me," Linda exclaimed almost angrily as she wiped the back of her hand across her cheeks. "I'm not normally this emotional at a Little League game."

Catherine squeezed her arm in reassurance. "You've got a right to be emotional. You miss your husband. I'd probably be a basket case."

"You?" Linda gasped in protest. "No way. You're so together, I can hardly believe it. Really. I wish I had your ability to organize my life."

Catherine's eyes drifted back to Michael, who was lining up his batters for the first inning. He moved among the boys with an ease and confidence that amazed her. It was as though he'd known them his whole life. "I'm starting to think that there's a lot more to life than being organized," she reflected almost to herself.

Linda followed her glance. "Your words or Michael's?"

"Mine," Catherine said firmly. But Michael had pried open the narrow confines of her life. "I guess there can be such a thing as being too absorbed in one's work."

Linda simply stared as though Catherine were a stranger. "Are you sure you're all right?" She placed a hand over Catherine's forehead. "No fever. But something has to be wrong—you haven't brought up the contract once and we've been sitting here almost fifteen minutes."

"You're right," Catherine realized with some astonishment. "And I don't intend to talk about work either."

"Well, I have to, then."

"Oh, no." Catherine groaned.

"Actually, I just need to ask a favor," Linda explained. "I've got a parent-teacher conference coming up for Mark next week and I can't get anybody to take my English Literature class. Could you?"

"No problem," Catherine answered without hesitation. "Just tell me where and when."

"You're a doll, Cathy."

Catherine leaned back in the stands with a satisfied smile. At one time, she would have told Linda that she had to check her calendar, talk to Marilyn, and rearrange her schedule before she could even consider taking over the lit class. But she had just discovered something. By being superefficient and superorgani-zed, she had succeeded only in isolating herself from other people, from the people who mattered to her. Granted, her career was important to her, but maybe she had let a few things slide—like friendship.

Linda was a teacher and mother, a woman separated from her husband for long periods of time. She needed a friend and, up until now, Catherine realized she'd only been a superficial acquaintance. A real friend would know about Mark's interest in Little League and show some sympathy for Linda's bouts of loneliness. A real friend didn't turn off her involvement when it stepped outside the boundaries of work.

"Come on, Mark. Hit it out of the park!" Linda screamed as her son stepped up to the plate.

Catherine heard the crack of the bat hitting the ball, and she found herself jumping up, shouting and hugging Linda as Mark slid into second base.

"Great hit," Catherine cried over the crowd's shouts.

"He's improved so much since Michael started coaching," Linda observed as they sat down again. "He was a real strikeout king before that. In fact, the whole team was kind of a washout. They hardly won any games, and only a few people ever attended."

"But look at all the people here tonight," Catherine swept her hand in front of her in a wide arc.

"That's now. Michael gave the team some spirit, and that rubbed off on the parents." Linda's voice was full of admiration. "He's really something."

*That's for sure,* Catherine agreed silently as they turned back to watch the game. Catherine joined into the spirit of the event and found herself enjoying every minute. She followed the score carefully, clapped when their team got a good hit or made a great play. She cheered for the boys until she was practically hoarse. And all through it, she never let her glance stray far from Michael. He seemed to be everywhere at once. He encouraged each boy with a smile or a pat on the back, whispered instructions when they were on base, and gave them pep talks when they sat on the bench. No wonder they were a winning team now. Michael knew how to make a person feel like a winner.

One last run in the final inning clinched the game for their team and everyone stampeded off the bleachers and swarmed onto the playing field to congratulate the boys. Catherine jumped down the steps with everyone else, and moved toward the group that had formed around Michael.

"Can you believe that Michael Moreno?" Catherine heard a woman say.

Two other women laughed in what seemed to Catherine like particularly irritating falsetto tones. "How can anyone be such a hunk and such a great guy with kids?"

"You said it," the first woman agreed with a little too much enthusiasm. "I even asked him if he would drive Johnny home tonight because I had to pick up my daughter at my ex's, and he agreed."

"Will you be waiting for him when he gets there?" one of the other two said in a suggestive tone.

"You better believe it." Her voice deepened to a low and vibrant note, and Catherine had to restrain herself from whirling around.

Just then, Michael caught sight of Catherine and motioned her over. As she approached him, her heart turned over at the sight of his hair tumbling over his forehead and his shirt clinging to his finely muscled chest. His eyes were almost hesitant as they met hers, but when he saw the shining excitement there, he took her hand and threaded his fingers tightly through hers. Catherine noted a small, dark-haired woman off to the side frown at that small gesture, and figured she must be Johnny's mother. Catherine couldn't resist smiling to herself at foiling the woman's plans of entrapment.

"I hope you weren't too bored," Michael murmured out of the corner of his mouth.

"Not at all. I loved every minute of it."

He squeezed her hand gratefully. Then he had to let go and shake hands with ecstatic parents who wanted to thank him. Michael modestly deflected all their praise, but he always made sure to add a few compliments about each person's son. It struck Catherine as odd that she had lived in Palm City her whole life and didn't know any of these people. Whereas Michael somehow had become part of the community and the residents' lives in only a few weeks. Suddenly, she could sympathize with the dark-haired woman's scheme to get Michael over to her house. She probably would have done the same thing in her place.

"Come on, let's go," Michael finally said as the crowd started to thin. "I hope you don't mind if Johnny Kennedy comes with us. His mother had a previous arrangement to be somewhere else, and I said I'd drop him off."

*If only you knew,* Catherine thought to herself with an inward grimace.

He interpreted her silence to be disappointment and leaned over to whisper in her ear. "At this moment I want to be alone with you more than anything, but..." His breath fanned her hair softly.

"We'll have time alone." Her voice was a soft murmur. "Later."

"Are we driving in this car?" Johnny asked, his eyes widening in amazement as they approached the pink Cadillac.

Michael laughed shortly. "I guess you've never seen a car like this, huh?"

"I'll say. It must be really old."

Michael's glance met Catherine's over the boy's head. There was a teasing glimmer in the sable depths of his eyes and she knew what was coming. "Yeah, they built them to last in those days." He ran a hand down one of the tail fins, but he was looking at Catherine when he spoke. "Anything built that year had class—sleek lines and beautiful curves."

Catherine's cheeks turned as pink as the car.

"Someday, I'd like to have a car like this," Johnny exclaimed as he climbed in the backseat.

"You can't buy one like this," Michael said, his eyes still on Catherine. "You have to want it with all your heart and then hope it finds you."

Catherine's heart took a perilous leap. "And when it does, what happens then?"

He moved closer to her. "Then you cherish it for the rest of your life."

His gaze traveled over her face and searched her eyes.

Her gaze lowered. What was he saying? She just wasn't sure. She hurried around to the other side of the car and slid in before he could say anything else that would cause her emotions to somersault.

"Come on, Mike, let's get going," Johnny urged with all the impatience of youth.

Michael stood there for a few moments, staring back at the baseball field without seeing it. Then he heaved a deep sigh. "Okay, partner."

As Michael drove out of the parking lot, he cursed himself inwardly. This hadn't been such a good idea. Their fun evening had suddenly turned serious. And what did he expect? He'd had a vague plan for the evening—take Catherine to the baseball game so she could relax and maybe let her guard down. Then take her for a casual dinner where he could subtly inquire about whether she was mismanaging money at the college? Stated that baldly, it sounded stupid, even juvenile.

What was the matter with his judgment? On the one hand he wanted her to enjoy herself tonight, but on the other hand he had to find out whether she was linked to some kind of conspiracy. And the whole time, all he really wanted to do was to be alone with her.

He was breaking his own rule of not getting involved.

He glanced over at her profile—the straight nose, curving cheeks, and firm chin. She turned at that moment and flashed him a shy smile that caused his heart to turn over. He gripped the wheel with renewed resolve. Maybe he'd lost all sense of perspective where she was concerned, but one thing he knew: She was not the type to do anything illegal. When he'd been an attorney in Miami, he'd met some of the slickest operators he could imagine. Some of them downright sleazy. And she was not that type at all.

Catherine might be ambitious and career-driven, but he'd stake his reputation on her honesty. In fact, he might have to do just that to get to the bottom of this mess.

"Mike, there's the Dock," Johnny's voice broke into his thoughts.

Michael blinked and signaled quickly to turn into the restaurant parking lot. "Sorry, I guess I was daydreaming."

"Thinking about how you won your game tonight?" Catherine asked softly.

"Yes, yes, I was." He was staring at her with an absent smile that told her he'd been thinking about something very different. But what?

"Come on, Johnny, let's buy Ms. Walker the specialty of the house," Michael enthused.

As they entered the long, low building jutting out into the Gulf of Mexico, Catherine realized the entire baseball team and their families were there. The open-air restaurant was practically vibrating with the same kind of excitement and energy that was present at the game. Michael waved at a few people as he took Catherine's arm and gently steered her over to a small table near the water.

"Mike, can I go sit with Tim and Gordon?" Johnny asked, pointing at a large table filled with about a dozen adults and children, all laughing and talking. As Michael looked over, he saw two young boys motioning Johnny over to the group.

"Okay, partner, but I take you home. I promised your mother." Michael playfully tipped the brim of Johnny's baseball cap.

As Johnny dashed over to the other table, Catherine watched him immediately become absorbed into the group. "It's amazing how kids just naturally come together. No awkwardness, no self-consciousness," she observed. Then she turned back to Michael with a smile. "And you're a natural. You work so well with the kids. I'm amazed."

"Why are you so surprised? I like kids. I always have." He watched Johnny elbow the boy next to him, who responded by giving him a light kick in the shins. Michael's mouth turned up slightly at their antics. "I'd like to have a family of my own someday."

"Boys to play ball with in the yard?" she inquired. She suddenly imagined small replicas of him—all with curling black hair and warm eyes. They'd be handsome little devils, just like their father.

"No, I think I'd like girls. Boys are too much trouble," he answered. He suddenly imagined miniature versions of

Catherine—all with soft blond hair and sky blue eyes. They'd be beautiful little angels, just like their mother.

Their gazes locked for a long moment and then they hastily looked away. "Where's that waitress?" they asked at the same time. They both laughed in embarrassment.

As if divining their question, a young waitress with a bouncing ponytail came up to the table. "Hi, Mike. What will it be tonight?"

"We'll have two of the specials, okay?" He glanced at Catherine, who nodded. "And I'll have a beer."

"Me too," Catherine added.

"Ms. Walker!" the young girl exclaimed. "Do you remember me?"

Catherine glanced uncertainly at the girl's wide eyes and freckled nose. Then she broke into an open, friendly smile of recognition. "Of course, Misty, I remember you. You were in my English Literature class two years ago. How are you doing?"

"Okay. I finish next year. This is my summer job, but it pays okay." She tossed her long brown ponytail over her shoulder. "I haven't seen you here before."

Catherine shrugged. "I've been pretty busy with my new job and everything."

"Yeah," Misty responded without much enthusiasm. "We were all sorry to see you give up teaching. You were a great teacher."

"Thanks."

The girl trotted off to get their food and drinks. Catherine felt a tiny glow inside at her former student's praise. She had a feeling of pride and self-confidence—a feeling she hadn't experienced once since taking on the administrative job. For a moment, she was back in the classroom, pacing energetically at the front, encouraging the students to give their opinions about a short story or poem they were reading.

"I guess I'm not the only one who's good with kids." Michael's observation broke into her thoughts.

Catherine laughed self-consciously. "Older ones— maybe, and only professionally, of course."

"I don't know. Misty seemed to admire you as a person just as much as a teacher." He bent his head slightly forward, capturing her eyes with his. "Why did you leave the classroom, Catherine? I just saw an expression on your face that I've never seen before. You seemed to light up like a candle when you were talking to Misty."

Catherine's glance slid away from his sharp eyes. She looked out over the calm evening waters of the Gulf. The sun was beginning to drop below the horizon, spreading a vivid red and orange sunset across the water like a curtain of fire. The night air was still, with only a hint of a breeze coming in softly with the tide.

But his question had stirred up feelings in her that were causing turbulent thoughts to surface. Why had she left teaching? Catherine's eyes turned pensive. She'd hardly let herself think about that since she'd taken on the administrative job. She blinked rapidly. There was really no need to think about it. It *had* been the right decision. "It was time to move on. An opportunity presented itself and I took it," she explained in a brusque voice.

"But was it the right opportunity?"

"Of course it was," Catherine almost snapped. "The classroom was a dead end. There was no chance of advancement or promotion. My mother always said it was a second-rate career choice to go into teaching, and she was right."

Michael watched as her features tightened, but he sensed her withdrawal was more of an emotional defense than a haughty justification. She was shutting him out because she couldn't look inside herself and find the answer. Hadn't he felt the same way himself when he'd been pursuing life in the fast lane in Miami and had no idea why?

Catherine shifted in her chair, uncomfortable with Michael's silence. "I've had to be a little ambitious— career-minded—to get ahead." She paused to clear her voice. "I may have let some things slide in my life—I see that now. But I've had to be single-minded. I'm on probation this year, and if I can't hack it, I'll be out of a job."

Michael nodded perfunctorily, but secretly he was relieved to hear her voice her uncertainty. Those weren't the words of someone who'd step over anybody and anything to get what she wanted, even if it meant doing something illegal. She was just worried that she couldn't make it as an administrator.

"I've been pushing pretty hard, but I'll slow down when the pressure eases up," she was saying. Suddenly, tears burned behind her eyes. But would the pressure ever ease up and, if it did, would she remember how to take back her life?

"Hey, I believe you." Michael reached out and squeezed her hand in reassurance. He wrapped his fingers tightly around hers, sending small tremors up her arm. "I've been there, remember? I was moving so fast in Miami, no one could keep up with me. I had the flashy cars, the penthouse on Biscayne Bay, and all the toys. My cases were high profile and I won every single one of them. Imagine. Just a boy from the migrant camps suddenly playing with the big guys. I didn't think anything would end my winning streak." Michael's mouth turned up in a smile of self-derision.

"Then everything fell apart?" Catherine asked gently.

Michael's laugh held a trace of self-mockery. "That's an understatement. I told you once that I wouldn't defend myself. Maybe that's because I'm partly to blame for my own fall. I should've seen it coming. I was set up, and the firm played on my arrogance and naïveté. I couldn't even believe that my fiancee, Felicia, might have been in on it."

His hand had tightened almost painfully around hers, but she barely noticed it. "Set up?"

"My partners arranged for me to take a case that ultimately resulted in my being accused of embezzlement," he was saying, his voice tight and clipped. "I think they knew this client was into illegal dealings and wanted to get rid of him, so I was the fall guy. Why not? I was just the junior partner and I was expendable." He paused. "So that was the end of my brief but illustrious career and my brief but not so illustrious engagement to Felicia."

"Michael, I'm so sorry," Catherine said in a gentle voice. Her heart ached for him. For once, he had dropped the easygoing demeanor to reveal something of the inner man, and she was affected deeply by the silent sadness of his face. "What did your parents say?"

"The one good thing about this whole mess is they weren't alive to see it." Michael's expression turned even more grim as he let loose of her hand. "They were killed in a car accident months before any of this happened. So they never knew their son had fallen from grace, so to speak."

He turned his head to look out over the water, and Catherine fell silent as she studied his dark-skinned profile. The set of his chin showed his stubborn streak, yet he had a humorous, kindly mouth that relieved his face from severity. The line from Byron came back to her: "He was bloody, but yet unbowed." Michael had come through the ordeal a little sadder, a lot wiser, but not cynical. He hadn't given up on people. If anything, the experience had made him more tolerant and more compassionate.

"You're a better person than I am, Michael Moreno," Catherine began. "I would've probably ended up soured on life after a betrayal like that."

Michael turned back to look at her, drinking in the image of her shining blue eyes and soft blond hair. "I can hardly picture you as a bitter recluse." But he couldn't let her go through what he had. Clenching his jaw with resolve, he knew he had to get to the bottom of this budget thing quickly and quietly, before anyone involved had a chance to set her up as a possible scapegoat.

Catherine shrugged lightly. "Maybe not a recluse. But certainly bitter. I've worked hard to get where I am now, and to see it all slip away would just about kill me."

"You underestimate yourself."

His words hummed in the air like the last chords of a symphony. They were straining to be heard, but Catherine shut her ears to them.

"Chili dogs and beer time," Misty practically sang as she placed two plates and two frosted beer mugs in front of them with a flourish.

"Great, thanks," Michael said warmly.

"Let me know if you need anything else," Misty reminded them before she moved away.

Catherine eyed her beer skeptically.

"Having second thoughts?" Michael teased. "Don't tell me you've never had a beer before?" As he watched a sheepish smile spread across her face, he gave an exclamation of disbelief. "Come on, everybody has had a beer."

"Not me," she confessed. "My mother never thought it was refined enough to drink at home, and since my dad was gone...." She left the rest of her thoughts unspoken.

"Well, Ms. Walker, your mother's not here and it's about time you let your hair down and joined the rest of us," Michael's voice was full of gaiety once more as he held up his mug.

He was right. Her mother wasn't here, watching and judging. Tonight was theirs.

Catherine raised her mug and they clinked the glasses together.

The evening had been pure magic, Catherine thought later as she nestled contentedly against the leather upholstery of Ruth's Cadillac.

She smiled at the contrast the Dock made with the elegant restaurants where Bill insisted on taking her for dinner. The Dock was casual, noisy, and cheap. Yet she had relished every bite of her chili dog and every swallow of her beer. She'd even let Michael dab the side of her mouth when the mustard had trickled down.

She couldn't remember what they'd talked about, but she remembered each and every expression that crossed his handsome face. His eyes glowed with a liquid brown fire as he talked about his work in education labor, and he gave that lopsided smile when she pressed him for more personal details about his life. In spite of the din that surrounded them, Catherine felt as if they were encircled by a magical web that insulated them from the people in the restaurant.

Not a single thing had spoiled the evening. Not even when they had dropped a sleepy Johnny off at his mother's house. Mrs. Kennedy had greeted Michael at the door wearing skin-tight leggings and a crop top. But once she caught sight of Catherine in the car, she retreated quickly back into the house with her son.

Catherine chuckled softly in the dark recesses of the car as she recalled the look of dismay on Mrs. Kennedy's face. Her little attempt to attract Michael had been foiled. Not that Catherine could really blame her for trying.

"What's so funny?" Michael's voice was a velvet murmur.

"Nothing." Catherine exhaled a long sigh of satisfaction as they drove along the palm-lined street that led to her house. Quietly swaying in the moonlight, the palm fronds cast fanlike shadows across the well kept lawns and the delicate scent of night-blooming jasmine floated through the air. "I was just thinking about what a wonderful evening it's been."

"Beer and a chili dog?" Michael probed with some amusement. "It's hardly wonderful. Not even second-class."

"Maybe that's what made it so great," Catherine said quietly. "We never went to places like that when I was a kid. Then when I was a teenager, I was always working so hard for good grades in school, I never had time to hang out. And now...."

"It doesn't fit the image of the up-and-coming exec?" Michael queried.

Catherine straightened abruptly, ready to snap back at him. But as she opened her mouth, she found she couldn't disagree with his comment. It was true. She couldn't deny it. She was glad he couldn't see the guilty blush that must have spread across her cheeks.

"Don't sweat it, Catherine. I've been there, remember?"

"What you must think of me," she murmured. "First, I treat you like a lackey at the gas station. Then, I come on like a stuffy, stiff-necked prig in our negotiations."

"Stiff, maybe. But stuffy, never," he reassured her with a hint of amusement in his voice.

Catherine laughed gently in spite of her embarrassment. She strained her eyes through the darkness to see him, but he remained a shadow. "You know, under that blue-collar exterior you're just a sweet, old-fashioned guy," she commented appreciatively.

"Oh, no," he said in pretended horror. "Don't tell anybody or my negotiating days will be over."

"It'll be our secret."

When they reached her house, Michael turned off the engine and the two of them sat staring out into the night in silence in the front seat of Ruth's Cadillac. The magical web that Catherine had perceived earlier was closing in around them, almost a palpable thing, weaving its spell.

Catherine quietly stepped out of the car and moved toward her house, with Michael following silently behind her. When she opened the front door, she stopped suddenly and slowly turned around. She stood frozen in the doorway. Her blue eyes glowed under the porch light and told him everything that she felt.

When he reached her, he gathered her into his arms in one forward motion and closed the door behind them.

## Chapter Eight

When Michael's lips touched hers, Catherine's arms slid around his neck as they stumbled together into the living room, his mouth never leaving hers. It felt so right. Everything else in the universe faded away, and it was just the two of them, entwined together, exploring a world of emotion where neither of them had been before.

Michael gently nuzzled Catherine's neck, inhaling the soft scent of roses that clung to her skin like a flower. "Catherine, I…" Michael faltered at a sudden clicking and printing sound. "What's that?"

Catherine glanced over her shoulder and then flipped on the living room light. "Just my fax machine."

"Oh, you have a fax. I hadn't noticed it before."

"I need it to hook into work…." She broke off, still too shaken to want to talk much. "I… I guess Bill is faxing the budget. He told me this afternoon that he'd have the documents faxed over here by this evening."

"What?" Michael quickly moved over to the fax machine. This was what he'd been waiting for. The sooner he cleared up the budget questions, the sooner he could face Catherine without any doubts or lies between them.

Hurt and dismay reflected in Catherine's eyes as she watched Michael's eager attention riveted on the fax machine, as if it were some kind of oracle. Only a few minutes ago he was holding her in a tender embrace, and now his heart was beating to the rhythm of the fax machine. Her mind reeled with confusion, trying to comprehend the sudden change in his mood.

"This is what I've been waiting for," Michael exclaimed as he ripped the last page of the budget off the machine. His eyes scanned over the pages for a few minutes. Then, as if suddenly remembering Catherine's presence, his eyes shifted back to her with an apologetic glance. "I've got to take this to Tallahassee as soon as possible, so I'll be gone a few days. I might not be back 'til Wednesday. Can we put a hold on the contract until then?"

"Sure," she said dully.

Michael came close, looking down at her intently. "I'll be back on Wednesday. Then we'll talk—and not about the contract." His hand traced the soft curve of her cheek, and the next moment he was gone.

Catherine stood there stunned for a few moments. She tried weighing the whole structure of events during the evening, but nothing added up to make any sense. Michael had bridged over the sea of all her fears and longings and then pulled back at the last moment. What had made him withdraw from her? Did he think she was another Felicia? A woman who couldn't be trusted with his heart?

But she would never leave him the way his ex-fiancee had. She couldn't—she loved him. Catherine slumped into the nearest chair. No, it wasn't possible. The thought froze in her brain. Did she really love him? Her mind could hardly register the surge of feeling from her heart, but she knew it was true. An even more shocking realization occurred to her—he obviously didn't love her.

After a restless weekend wrestling with the knowledge of her love for Michael and irritation over his absence, Catherine sat hollow-eyed and listless at her desk on Monday morning. Marilyn had drifted in and out with maintenance requisition forms for her to sign, and Catherine barely registered what she put her signature on. All she could think about was Michael. Why wouldn't he be back until Wednesday? And what did he want to talk about? She shivered both in anticipation and apprehension.

"Did you get the budget I faxed to you on Friday?" Bill cut into her thoughts as he breezed into her office around mid morning. He was wearing his usual brown suit and smug expression.

"Yes, I did," Catherine said in a cool voice, leaving no doubt that she was not in a talking mood. She hoped Bill would take the hint and leave. But when he lingered, she continued even more abruptly, "Look, I'm really busy this morning, so if there's nothing else...." She left the rest of the sentence unspoken, but her intent was clear—to anyone except a man as thick-skulled as Bill.

"You know," he began, "I was really mad at you Friday. I couldn't believe you stood me up."

"I was hardly standing you up—"

"We had a date and you didn't show."

"Bill—"

He was waving his hand back and forth in a gesture of dismissal. "It doesn't matter, because I now know what you were up to."

"Up to? Did I miss something?"

He swaggered over to her desk, hitched up his pant leg, and seated himself comfortably on the smoothly polished corner of her desk. "I heard about you and Moreno last Friday—at a Little League game, of all things. I wish I could've been there to see that." He snickered.

"It wasn't so bad," she said defensively.

"Hey, I know we've got to make these little personal sacrifices to get what we want—and I approve."

"Approve?" Catherine was more baffled than ever. Was Bill having a complete breakdown?

"Of getting in with Moreno—for the contract, of course." Bill's sandy-colored eyes reflected glimmers of cold-hearted satisfaction. "Only you would have the smarts to insinuate yourself with that Harvard smart aleck to get to know his weaknesses before you lower the boom." He paused, pursing his lips. "I love it."

Catherine felt sick. How could Bill possibly think she'd be capable of such vicious duplicity? Did he see her as such a low, amoral person? A hot denial rushed to her lips, but then she stopped herself. To deny it would only reveal how she felt about Michael—and her feelings were definitely not appropriate. Then, too, Bill had the ear of the president. Dr. Cramer could make her life uncomfortable, to say the least.

If only she knew where she stood with Michael, but she hadn't even had so much as a phone call from him. Wouldn't Bill laugh at that—to know how vulnerable she really was.

Her eyes turned a murky blue as she fixed Bill with a hard stare. "How clever of you to figure it all out."

"I didn't get where I am by being stupid," he boasted as an unpleasant smile sliced across his face.

*No, you got there by bootlicking every boss you've ever had,* Catherine countered silently.

Bill heaved himself off her desk. He flicked an imaginary piece of lint off his sleeve. "Don't let Moreno down too easily when you're done with him, Cathy. I'd like to see him squirm a little."

"Why?"

"He usurped my Friday-night date."

Catherine smiled weakly.

As he exited, Marilyn suddenly appeared at her door. Her secretary's normally composed features momentarily broke into a stare of pure dislike toward Bill as he brushed past her. How much of their conversation had Marilyn heard? Catherine thought in sudden alarm.

"President Cramer on line two," Marilyn announced in a frosty voice that left no doubt as to whether she had overheard Catherine's conversation with Bill.

"Marilyn—"

"I wouldn't keep him waiting. You know how impatient he gets," Marilyn reminded her with a sidelong glance of disillusionment and disbelief.

"But Marilyn—" She was already gone.

Catherine groaned in frustration. Surely Marilyn didn't think that she had been telling Bill the truth about lying to Michael? That sounded convoluted, even to her own ears. She was getting helplessly mired deeper and deeper into this subterfuge with every passing minute. And now the president wanted to talk to her. That was always a treat.

Catherine reluctantly picked up the phone.

"How is everything going, Catherine?" Dr. Cramer asked in a pleasant voice.

"Fine." Catherine's grasp tightened on the phone, anticipating the president's usual biting criticism.

"I heard negotiations had been suspended for a few days."

"Yes. Apparently, Mr. Moreno had some business to attend to, so we agreed to resume negotiations on Wednesday." Catherine kept her tone carefully neutral. She didn't know why she had neglected to inform him that Michael had dashed off to Tallahassee as soon as he had the budget in hand. Something told her that the president wouldn't like that one bit.

"No need to explain, Catherine. You've been working very hard the last few weeks and a little break will do you good," he answered indulgently.

Catherine's mouth dropped open. She could hardly believe it. The president was actually expressing concern for her. He had never shown any warmth or understanding to her before, so why was he acting so caring now? "I've enjoyed the negotiations. You know how much I like to tackle a tough project," she responded with her old war song. But it rang hollow in her ears. The only reason she'd enjoyed working on the contract was because of Michael. She'd had the opportunity to be near him, get to know him, and—yes—to learn to love him.

"Glad to hear it." The president paused for a few moments and cleared his throat lightly. "Did Moreno get the budget?"

"Yes. He's looking it over."

"Good, good Did he say anything about it?"

Dr. Cramer asked in a smooth voice.

"Nothing special." Catherine thought she detected a note of hesitation behind his words, and that baffled her. It was so out of character for him. He was always aggressive and confident about getting what he wanted.

"He didn't have any questions about expenditures?" the president inquired further.

"We haven't really had time to talk about it," Catherine confessed. "But I'm sure we'll get into it when he returns and we start negotiating again."

"Yes, of course. You'll tell me if he has any questions."

"Certainly."

"Right then. I'll be speaking with you in a day or two." He hung up abruptly.

Catherine lowered the phone from her ear and stared speechless at the receiver for a few moments before she hung up. That was the strangest conversation she'd ever had with Dr. Cramer. She'd heard him chew out employees when he was ripping mad, she'd heard him smooth over a deal with other businessmen, but she'd never heard him sound unsure of himself. Was there something going on that she didn't know about? But what could shake up a man with the kind of supreme ego of President Cramer?

"Ms. Walker?" Marilyn appeared at the door, interrupting Catherine's musings. "I'm going for lunch now."

Marilyn started to turn around when Catherine exclaimed, "What, Marilyn. Will you come in please and close the door?"

Her secretary shifted from foot to foot. Then she moved forward and closed the door behind her. Her eyes were fastened on the gray and rose patterned carpet on Catherine's office floor.

"Marilyn," Catherine began, taking a deep breath. She had to take the chance and confide in her. "I don't know what you heard a little while ago—between Bill and me, that is. But it wasn't what it appeared to be."

Marilyn continued to regard the carpet silently.

"Look, I know I probably shouldn't say this, but I was on an honest-to-goodness date with Michael Moreno last Friday. We went to a Little League game and then had dinner." Catherine's words came out in a tumbled rush. Just talking about their date sent waves of excitement through her. "I guess I thought if I told Bill the truth he'd accuse me of compromising the negotiations. And there's no telling what he might try to do to upset everything," she added.

Marilyn sighed in relief as she finally looked at Catherine. "I knew you wouldn't do the kind of thing Mr. Myers suggested."

"You never doubted me?"

"Never."

Catherine's delicate brows rose skeptically.

"Well, maybe for just a moment or two," Marilyn confessed. A ghost of a smile turned up the corners of her mouth.

"Understandable," Catherine murmured, half to herself. "I haven't been the most likable boss. In fact, I guess I've been pretty snooty. But it doesn't mean I don't appreciate everything you do, Marilyn. You've smoothed over a lot of rough edges for me," she said in frank gratitude. "I have a lot to learn about being an administrator, and I hope I can make your job a little more pleasant from now on."

Marilyn's cheeks turned pink with pleasure. "Thank you, Ms. Walker."

"And let's drop the Ms. Walker. My name is Catherine."

"Whatever you say." Marilyn was practically beaming now.

After a brief pause, Catherine said slowly, "Just between you and me, I don't know what's going to happen after this contract business is over. Michael has become…well…more than just a colleague to me."

The two women exchanged a glance, and Catherine felt her heart must surely have shown in her eyes, because Marilyn just nodded in understanding.

"You can count on me—no matter what," Marilyn assured her in a firm voice.

Catherine smiled. "Thanks. I may need it."

"You've got it." Marilyn turned to exit from Catherine's office, but then she added an afterthought. "Michael is such a great guy. You'd make a wonderful couple."

Once her secretary closed the door, Catherine's smile instantly faded. She slumped forward, her arms bent, propping up her chin in her hands. "Oh, Michael, where are you? I need you."

Michael was driving south through the central part of Florida the next afternoon. He whizzed by mile after mile of lush orange groves without even taking notice of their beauty or smelling the sweet perfume of their fruit. Instead, he concentrated grim-faced on the road in front of him.

The last few days in Tallahassee had shaken him to the core.

# A Labor of Love

Harry had been waiting for him on Saturday morning along with John Kent, a budget expert. As the three of them began to go through an item-by-item analysis of expenditures, it rapidly became clear that there was money unaccounted for—a large sum of money, in fact.

"Mike, this smells rotten," was the way Harry had phrased it.

They spent all weekend breaking down each category of expenditure until they finally found the area with the unaccounted-for money.

"By the saints, they've been doing some hanky-panky with the maintenance funds," Harry had exclaimed, slapping his thigh.

"How original," John Kent had added drily.

Michael took in a quick, sharp breath.

"Yes, it looks like almost two hundred thousand dollars has been funneled through maintenance expenditures, but there aren't any specific renovations on the college buildings listed on the other documents." Harry sifted through the pages of the budget and then threw them down on the table in disgust.

"That means one thing," John pointed out with a thin smile.

"Somebody's getting a little private work done— off campus," Harry finished for him.

"Who do you think is involved?" Michael asked slowly.

"Who do you think?" Harry smiled. "The big man himself. It just so happens that we've got ten reports indicating that President Cramer has had quite a bit of work done on his house recently, including a twenty-five-thousand-dollar swimming pool."

"It'll be easy enough to prove if he's had the renovations done," Harry pointed out. "But we have to know who signed the official college requisition forms for the work, or Dr. Cramer can say he paid for the renovations himself."

"Who's responsible for authorizing maintenance work?" John turned toward Michael.

"I... I'm not sure." Michael hesitated.

Harry's stare drilled into Michael. "Isn't it Catherine Walker?"

"Possibly," Michael said reluctantly.

"Look, Mike," Harry continued, his stare still fixed. "We've got to get to the bottom of this mess immediately. The negotiations will be meaningless if they're based on a falsified budget."

"And we need to see the requisition forms before we can take any further action or make any statements," John added.

"You're not suggesting that Catherine is involved in this in any way?" Michael demanded angrily, but in his heart he wondered.... She *was* the one who signed the requisition forms.

Harry flung his hands out, palms up. "I don't know. But we've got to find out one way or the other." He paused. Then his voice hardened. "You can't let your feelings get in the way of your work. You've got to find out who's involved. For goodness' sake, Mike, we're not talking about petty cash here. The college's funds are being embezzled."

"I know. I know." Mike ran a hand through his thick, dark hair in frustration.

"She may be in on it, true. But let me point out another scenario," John interjected in a calm voice. "She may have been put in that job as a buffer to take the heat. She signs the requisition forms and, therefore, is set up as the fall guy if things go wrong. If the forms are mysteriously missing, she still takes the fall for incompetence. The president wins because there's no paperwork to indicate the work on his house was paid for by the college."

"Quite possible," Harry concurred. "It's clever and may be foolproof, even if it's not very original. From what I know about Cramer, I wouldn't put it past him."

Michael listened, but he was also thinking rapidly about the course of action he would have to take. He could confront Cramer with the evidence, but the president would probably only deny everything and then accuse Catherine of incompetence—or worse. Michael could request the college maintenance records, but that could arouse Cramer's suspicions— and again he might try to frame Catherine. The only thing Michael knew for certain was that he couldn't let her take the fall. She might be anxious to get on the fast track to success, but she wasn't dishonest. He knew it as sure as he knew he was innocent of what he'd been accused of seven years ago.

"Mike?" Harry voice held a question. "We've got to move on this fast. I want Cramer out before he can do any more damage."

"Let me handle it, okay?" Mike asked, his tone full of entreaty. "I'll find out who's behind this conspiracy and I'll get the documentation we need to support our case."

"No matter where it leads or who it implicates," Harry reminded him, a warning in his voice.

"I know my job." That had been Michael's parting comment.

But was he really so sure that he could remain impartial? What if the facts did implicate Catherine? *How could she defend herself?* Michael asked himself for the hundredth time as he continued to replay the events of the weekend. He gripped the steering wheel tightly as he remembered Harry's dubious look when Michael said he'd do his job—no matter what.

Did they believe him? They agreed to let him come back to Palm City to investigate. They trusted him that much. But did he trust himself?

All he could see was Catherine's face, her blue eyes melting under his, her soft cloud of blond hair curving to her shoulders.

A horn honked and Michael realized he had stopped at a traffic light and it was now green. He pressed down the gas pedal and shook his head, trying to clear his mind of Catherine's image.

He just couldn't let her be hung out to dry by her boss. Michael believed in her. She wasn't the kind of person who'd knowingly enter into anything illegal. But it was possible she didn't know what she was signing. Could she have been duped into doing something without her knowledge?

Michael pounded the wheel with his right hand and pressed the gas pedal down even farther. He had to get to Palm City. He had to find the truth. Her career depended on it and his career depended on it. But more than that was motivating him. He wanted to do it for her. More than anything, Michael wanted to protect Catherine, to stand by her. He had to. He loved her.

# Chapter Nine

By the time Michael arrived at Palm City Community College, it was late afternoon. He'd mentally rehearsed a dozen plans about how to approach Catherine, none of which seemed right, and his head was still swirling with doubts. But he had to tell her. He had to give her a chance to explain why two hundred thousand dollars was missing in the budget.

As he strode around the corner toward Catherine's office, he almost knocked Marilyn down.

"Excuse me, Marilyn," he apologized as he grasped her arm to steady her.

"My fault. I was in a rush." She hitched her purse strap back up on her shoulder.

"Is Catherine still in?"

"She's teaching Linda Fisher's lit class in Bingly Hall two hundred and three." Marilyn glanced at her watch. "It should be over in about fifteen minutes."

"Thanks." An idea suddenly occurred to him. "I just might sit in, if you don't think she'd mind."

"Oh, I don't think she'd mind at all."

Why was Marilyn smiling in that oddly benign manner? Michael wondered. "Okay, then. I'll just go on over."

Marilyn's smile broadened. "See you."

"Right." He turned and started back down the hall. As he glanced over his shoulder, he saw that Marilyn was still smiling. What was going on with *her* now? Michael gave an impatient shrug. This place was getting crazier by the minute. Money had disappeared. People were acting strange. And he was looking for answers to all of this nuttiness. He must be crazy himself to put his reputation on the line like this. He was hardly in a position to have another dark spot on his record. So why was he risking everything?

*For Catherine,* a voice whispered inside. *It was all for her.*

As Michael slowly opened the door to the classroom, he heard her voice and he knew he had made the right decision. She was worth risking everything for. He quietly slipped into a chair in the back of the room, noting how the other students barely registered his entrance. They were all intently watching Catherine, who stood at the blackboard.

As his glance traveled toward the front of the room, his eyes met hers, causing an almost physical impact. How could he have spent the last four days separated from her? It had been an eternity. He wanted to take her in his arms here and now and see if her kiss was as sweet as he remembered.

Catherine stumbled slightly over her words when she caught sight of Michael, but she quickly recovered. They exchanged a subtle look of amusement, but no one else in the room appeared to have noticed. The students were too caught up in what Catherine was saying.

"What do you think Shakespeare meant in this sonnet by the idea that his mistress's eyes 'were nothing like the sun' or that 'every fair from fair declines'?" she asked the class.

The class was silent for a few moments.

"Shakespeare was saying that his girlfriend wasn't the most spectacular babe of all time," a young man in the back of the room piped up.

The other students laughed and Catherine smiled. "Not bad. I don't know that Shakespeare would use the word babe, but that's definitely what he's saying. Maybe his mistress wasn't the most beautiful woman, but—" She paused.

"She's beautiful in his eyes," a young woman with glasses finished for Catherine.

"Exactly." She nodded in encouragement. "And what about the line 'summer's lease hath all too short a date'? What happens to the beauty of youth?"

"We get older," another woman in the front answered. "And we lose it."

"Yes. Hopefully, it doesn't all go at once," Catherine quipped and the whole class laughed.

As Catherine continued drawing the students out, Michael sat there amazed at the transformation in the woman he loved. She strode confidently around the room, encouraging each student with a small nod or words of praise, until almost every student was participating in the discussion. And Catherine accomplished this task in a seemingly effortless manner. There was none of the tenseness or stiffness that she projected in her office. She simply glowed.

She even looked different. For once she hadn't donned one of her usual business-armor suits. She wore a flowing red silk dress decorated with tiny black flowers. It swirled around her soft waves as she moved around the room.

Catherine was born to teach. Michael could see that after five minutes of watching her with the students. And, what's more, she seemed to revel in it. So why had she left what she liked to do for a job that caused her continual discontent and stress?

"So if Shakespeare is saying his mistress isn't the most beautiful woman in the world and she isn't the most perfect woman in the world, why does he love her?" Catherine challenged her class, her eyes sweeping over the group.

No one answered for a few moments as Catherine continued to glance around the room. "What do you think? Do we love only perfect people?"

"We love people in spite of their imperfections," Michael found himself saying. Many students turned around to look at him, but he only had eyes for Catherine. And there was a double meaning behind his words that he wanted her to understand. "That's what it means to love—to accept the whole package, flaws included."

His words sent Catherine's heart spinning. Was he saying that he loved her, in spite of the way she'd acted when they first met? In spite of her haughtiness during their negotiations?

"But then why do people always say they have this ideal of a perfect guy or girl?" the young woman with glasses inquired.

"It's only natural to hope you will meet someone perfectly suited to you. But perhaps after falling in love, you'll stop worrying about perfection, because even flaws are lovable then," Catherine went on, causing a swell of exclamations from the other students. But she didn't sort out the comments. She was still looking at Michael. Could he see that she was trying to say that she loved him?

Catherine gave herself a mental shake. She had to stay focused on the class.

"I think there's too much emphasis on looks all-together," the young man in the back offered. "It makes it tough for guys like me—"

"To pick up a spectacular babe?" Catherine finished for him.

The whole class burst into laughter.

After a few moments of joining in, Catherine looked down at her watch. "Well, I think that's about it for this afternoon." A note of regret touched her voice. As she scanned over the eager young faces in the class, she felt a deeper pang inside.

# A LABOR OF LOVE

It felt so good to be back in the classroom again, talking about literature and generating ideas. She'd slipped back into her role of teacher without the slightest bit of awkwardness. It was so natural. It was like coming home to a place that she'd put out of her mind, but never quite forgot. It felt right.

"I'll tell Ms. Fisher that we finished the Shakespeare sonnet," Catherine said to the class. "Great discussion."

"Thanks, Ms. Walker," the students murmured as they trailed out.

When the last student had left, Michael still remained in his seat in the back of the room. Catherine gathered up her books and fumbled with her purse, unable to look directly at Michael. For some reason, with the students gone, she had lost some of her bravado about revealing her feelings to Michael. The room was deadly quiet.

He raised his hand. "I have a question, Ms. Walker."

She set her books back down. "Yes?"

"Was Shakespeare right?"

"About what?"

"Love conquering all."

Catherine faltered. "I... I'm not sure."

Michael rose and weaved a path around the jumbled desks toward her. He halted when he was but inches away from her. "I missed you," he said quietly, almost without emotion.

But as he looked down at her, the ardor in his brown eyes could have melted a frozen tundra. Tenderness and love were all there in his words and in his face. Catherine's smile broke through like sunlight after a storm and she wondered if he could see right into her own heart. "I missed you too."

Catherine ached to ask him if he'd been as miserable as she had. If he'd spent every hour wondering what she was doing, as she had about him. But as she noticed the tiredness around his eyes and the hint of stubble on his cheeks, she knew she didn't have to ask.

"I need to tell you something," Michael began, his low voice a little awkward.

Catherine smiled to herself. Of course he'd feel awkward. She had given him a hard time during the last few weeks and there were still unanswered questions between them. But they would sort them out. They would find a common ground to establish their relationship on. She felt sure of it. Once he said he loved her, nothing would stand between them.

"Catherine, I don't know how to tell you this." He took her by the arms, and she thrilled at his touch.

"Just say it, Michael," she urged.

"Okay." He dropped his hands suddenly and moved back from her. He had to keep some distance between them or he wouldn't be able to think straight. Looking down into those pale but proud features and melting blue eyes, he felt an overpowering urge to take her in his arms and carry her away from anything that threatened her. It was such a strong feeling. In that moment, he knew what it felt like to want to fight the world to protect the woman he loved.

But Catherine wouldn't want him to take her away from it all. Everything she cared about was here—her job was here. And she'd fight to keep it.

Michael took a deep breath. "When I was in Tallahassee this weekend, I spent some time going over the college budget with two financial experts from the union. We found some...problems."

"Problems?" She had expected him to say something sweet and personal. Something about love. What did the budget have to do with anything?

"I don't know how to say this, and technically I shouldn't even be telling you, but I want to give you the opportunity to defend yourself if—"

"What? Why should I have to defend myself to anyone?"

He seemed to hesitate. "Maybe that wasn't a good choice of words. I need to get at the truth and I hope you're the person who can explain."

Catherine backed farther away from him until she thumped against the blackboard. Michael was not declaring his love at all; he was accusing her of something. She fought down the hysteria that suddenly bubbled up inside, making her want to erupt in wild laughter at her own foolishness. Michael didn't love her. He was simply her opponent at the negotiating table. But *something* had passed between them. Hadn't it? She wasn't imagining it, was she? Her mind was spinning like a carousel out of control, and she clutched the chalk tray behind her in an effort to keep her balance.

"I... I'm not sure what you're talking about, Michael," she finally managed to get out in a slow, deliberate voice.

There was only one way, Michael realized. He had to just spit it out. "There's almost two hundred thousand dollars in the budget that has been...well...misappropriated. This money was supposedly spent on maintenance at the college, but there's no record of the construction or renovation work ever having taken place." His expression turned even more somber. "But there are apparently rumors that Dr. Cramer had expensive work done on his home—very expensive renovations on his very upscale house on the Gulf."

"I don't believe it," Catherine said, incredulous.

"It's true. Someone has been approving expenditures for work not done at the college. And since you're the one who signs the forms. ..." Michael's voice trailed off on a note of unmistakable finality. "The budget doesn't lie."

"But I do. Is that what you're saying?" Catherine asked in a choked voice. "You think I've been hiding this from you, hoping you wouldn't find out the truth?"

"No, no—"

Tears sprang to her eyes as she heaved herself upright again. "That's what you're saying, isn't it? That I've been in on some kind of conspiracy to cheat the college out of money. The president and me, right? Two big-time embezzlers." Her voice rose an octave as she paced erratically across the room.

"I never said that about you, Catherine," Michael protested hotly. "If I believed that, why would I be telling you all of this? I could've just given the information to a state attorney and let him investigate."

She gave an exclamation that sounded like a sob. "Why don't you? I can't believe what a fool I've been. All this weekend I've been thinking about you, missing you, and you've been plotting against me."

Michael's hand gripped her firmly by the wrist. "That's not true and you know it."

"Do I?" Catherine tried to pull her hand out of his grip, but he only increased the pressure. "You're accusing me of stealing money. What do you expect? That I should thank you?"

"Credit me with a little concern for your feelings. I drove all day like a madman to get here so I could talk to you—"

"And I'm supposed to be grateful that you accused me in person?" Catherine laughed in a harsh, raw voice. "Well, thanks for nothing. With friends like you, I don't need enemies. In fact, I don't need you at all. You don't care about me. You're just the man who sits across from me at the negotiating table," she blazed at him. She pushed at his chest, but when he wouldn't let go of her wrist, she balled her other hand into a fist and hammered at his chest. "Let me go, darn it!"

"No, I won't let you go." Michael's strong hands caught hers and circled them around her back as he stilled her flailing arms. In one forward motion, she was brought up against his chest, unable to move. "Catherine, please, calm down. I can't talk to you when you're trying to punch me out."

She struggled for a few more moments and then stopped, defeated.

"Will you listen to me?"

She nodded mutely.

"Cathy?"

"All right. I'll listen." She tried to calm the erratic rhythm of her breathing.

He wanted desperately to bend his head the few inches that separated them and let his mouth brush hers, let his kiss tell her everything in his heart. Instead, he dropped his arms and let her go.

Catherine stepped back and crossed her arms across her chest. "So?"

Michael stood there watching her, feeling the tension emanating from her body. Instead of clearing the air, her outburst served only to cloud the issue that hung between them like a dark specter. "First, I want you to understand that I'm not accusing you of anything, okay?"

She was silent for a few moments. "Okay," she said carefully.

She heard his sharp breath of relief before he continued. "Like I said before, the maintenance funds show a debit of about two hundred thousand dollars that can't be accounted for."

"But how can that be?"

"Normally, any construction or renovations are itemized in the budget. So the amount allocated for maintenance funds should equal the total of all the itemized work done at the college. But it doesn't. Once all the items are added up, the total doesn't come anywhere near the money allocated."

"Could the money have been placed in another category? Like scholarships or books for the library?" Catherine asked with a tinge of desperation in her voice.

He shook his head. "Maintenance money comes out of special state funds. It can't be transferred."

131

His words shattered her last shred of hope, and her chin dropped down to her chest in defeat. "It's true, then."

Michael swore under his breath. He'd make that jerk Cramer pay for the pain he was making Catherine suffer if it was the last thing he did. "Are you all right?"

"I... I don't know. It's all so difficult to believe. But I do know that I'd remember signing any requisition that was so high....I mean, I wouldn't sign it at all." She couldn't look at him. She didn't want to see the pity in his eyes. "It's so much money. How could it just disappear like that?"

"That's where I'm hoping you can help."

Catherine looked up, startled. "What do you mean?"

Michael's jaw tightened. "If I confront Dr. Cramer with our evidence of misappropriated funds, what do you think he'll do?"

"Why...I guess he'd try to build a case to show that he's innocent of any wrongdoing."

"And where would he go?"

"He'd probably start by getting hold of the maintenance requisition forms that I—" She broke off, meeting his questioning gaze with dawning realization.

"That you have authorized," he finished for her.

"But I don't think there are any forms that show that amount of money—" Catherine covered her mouth in horror. "Oh, no."

"You've got it," Michael said grimly. "If there is no documentation to show the work was authorized, he can simply say the forms were lost due to your incompetence. He's off the hook, the money can't be traced, and since you're responsible for accounting for the forms. ..."

"Don't say it," Catherine exclaimed.

Her shocked expression made Michael want to wring Cramer's neck.

"I can't believe what a fool I've been," Catherine said bitterly. "I thought I got my job because of my qualifications. I thought the president really respected me, but all the time he was just setting me up for this...this scam."

"That's not true," Michael insisted in a firm voice. "You deserved your job, and you've done it well. It's just that Cramer and his type *use* people."

She balled her hands at her sides. "I am *not* giving up without a fight, I'll tell you that. I've worked hard to get where I am, and I haven't done anything wrong. He's not bringing me down with him."

Michael watched her with growing admiration in his eyes. "That's the spirit, Cathy. We'll beat him at his game."

"It won't be easy, will it?"

"Probably not."

Catherine turned to him, her chin set resolutely. "What do we do first?"

"Do you have copies of all the maintenance requisition forms?"

She nodded. "In my office files."

"Good. Let's get over there now. We'll go through them one by one—all night if we have to. Something might show up."

She took a deep breath. "Okay. You go on. I need a few minutes alone to compose myself. All this has been almost too much to take in."

He reached for her and planted a soft kiss on her forehead. "I'll go over to your office and wait for you. We'll find a way out of this, I promise you."

When he was gone, Catherine's eyes clouded with fear and doubt. Was there any way out? Or was her career finished? The career she'd worked a lifetime to build. And when it was over, would Michael want to have anything to do with her? The last thing he needed as he rebuilt his own career was a woman who'd been fired for incompetence. What was she going to do?

As Michael watched Catherine stride into her office a few minutes later, he almost applauded in admiration. She had smoothed down her hair, repaired her makeup, and squared her chin in determination. She had obviously made up her mind to fight this thing. Never had he felt such love for her as that moment. She was not the type of woman who would ever accept defeat, no matter what the odds. She was not another Felicia. She would stand up for what she believed in, and maybe even for the man she loved.

She yanked open the top drawer of her file cabinet and pulled out a large stack of folders. She then plopped them on the conference table, where the two of them had been negotiating the contract the last few weeks. "Let's get started." Her eyes met his defiantly. "What are we looking for?

"Any large expenditures that you might not have noticed when—"

"As I said, I'd notice two hundred thousand dollars," Catherine said drily.

"It wouldn't have been done all at once," Michael pointed out as he slipped off his jacket and turned up his shirtsleeves. "Items have probably been slipped in and attached to other expenditures. So if you find a typical expenditure that seems high, it might've been padded, and that's what we're looking for."

"These are the requisition forms for the entire year, so the answer has got to be here somewhere." Catherine jammed herself into a chair and snapped the files open. "We've got to find it."

He reached over and covered her hand with his. "We will."

She gasped lightly and almost lost control for a moment, but the solid strength of his fingers was urging yet protective. She gave a forced smile and a tense nod of consent. "I *know* we will," she said in a firm voice.

Hours later, those words reverberated through Catherine's mind as stupidly optimistic. They had spent the day going through every single requisition form and could find nothing, absolutely nothing, that indicated anything was amiss with the maintenance funds.

"It's not here. Whatever we're looking for, it's just not here," Catherine croaked wearily as she stared at the mass of forms spread across the table. Her hair fell forward in a tumbled mess and she shoved it impatiently behind her ears.

Michael leaned back in his chair and rubbed his red-rimmed eyes. "Maybe you're right."

"It's hopeless, then." Her voice was devoid of all emotion. "If we can't find anything to show the bills were padded, then how can we make a case against Dr. Cramer?"

"I don't know." He tilted his head forward and massaged the back of his neck, trying to think. "What time is it?"

"Almost four-thirty."

No wonder he couldn't think straight. He'd been up almost four nights straight with only a few hours' sleep. But he had to think clearly. He had to help Catherine. "How about some more coffee?"

"Michael, go home," Catherine said quietly. "There's nothing more that you can do."

His head snapped back up instantly. "I'm not leaving."

She flung out her hands in simple despair. "This isn't your fight. It's mine, and I don't know what else to do. Maybe I can't fight Cramer. He's covered his tracks very well, and without proof of his wrongdoing, I've got nothing to protect me."

"You've got me."

She closed her eyes to hide the tears that suddenly threatened to spill down her face. "I don't want to pull you down with me, Michael. I don't think I should accept your help."

"Well, you've got it whether you want it or not," he insisted. He stood up abruptly and slammed both fists down on the table, scattering the piles of paper. "I'm not a quitter. And I'm not going to let you face this alone."

Catherine became instantly wide-awake and dry-eyed. "Michael—"

"No, you listen to me, Cathy." He sliced the air with an impatient hand. Leaning across the table, his dark eyes suddenly turned wild. "You think you can handle everything by yourself, that you don't need anybody. I thought that once and I paid the price for it. I wouldn't accept one favor. I was too proud to ask for help and guess what? Nobody lifted a finger to help me, and I took a fast trip down the tubes."

"This isn't the same thing," Catherine protested, taken aback by the bitterness in his voice.

"Isn't it?" He laughed mirthlessly.

"Besides." She cleared her throat. "I thought you said that you had put all that behind you. That it was all in the past."

After an interminable moment he said, "Sure. I didn't want to remember how much it hurt. But betrayal is never really forgotten. It cuts deep. That's why I'm going to be here for you, Catherine."

Catherine studied her hands, suddenly bereft of words. She was struck by his admission. Could it be that his emotions ran deeper than she ever suspected? Did he feel that deeply about her as well?

Michael straightened and, with a jerking movement, jammed his fists deeply into his pockets. He looked at her intently, then strode over to the window. He stared out at the starless black of the night sky and then wheeled back toward her. The ghost of his lopsided grin appeared on his face. "Funny, isn't it?"

"What?" Her throat was dry.

"I tried so hard to pretend that I didn't care—about anything. And now here I am caring so much, I can hardly stand it."

Catherine swallowed hard, trying to keep her voice from shaking. "What...what is it you care about?"

The room fell into a hushed silence as Catherine waited breathlessly for his answer.

His expression darkened again. "I care about not letting someone like Cramer win. His type always wins." He paused, his eyes clouding with memories of the past. "Maybe if I can stop him, it'll make up for what happened to me somehow. Those so-called partners of mine got away scot-free after destroying my career, but I'm not going to let Cramer do the same thing to you and get away with it."

Catherine dropped her lashes quickly to hide her sense of hurt. But then a twinge of guilt added to her disappointment. He wasn't just doing this for himself; he was doing it for her too. What more could she ask for? *For him to say he's doing it because he loves me,* a tiny voice added inside.

"Michael, you forget. We've been at this for hours and we're no closer to finding the truth than when we first started," Catherine reminded him, a weary note creeping back into her voice.

Michael hesitated. Then something disturbing replaced the murkiness in his eyes. His smile was anything but pleasant as he drove his right fist into the palm of his left hand again and again. "I've got one more idea—and it just might work."

Alarm spread through Catherine like wildfire. She didn't like the look on his face or the suggestion of violence behind his words. "Michael, don't do anything rash. You're on edge and not thinking clearly. Maybe you need to take a little rest. Then we can plan in the morning—"

"No, there's something I've got to do."

"Michael," she exclaimed. The tone of her voice must have touched him, because an emotion akin to tenderness broke through his grim expression.

"Don't worry. I won't do anything to hurt your reputation."

"I don't care about that," she cried from the heart. "I don't want *you* to be hurt."

"I know," he said fiercely, taking her by the arms and pulling her close to him. All the feelings he'd bottled up for days rose to the surface as their lips met. It was a kiss of desperation yet it was also a pledge of his loyalty and love.

As Michael pulled back, his ragged breathing was the only sound in the room. He started to say something, but then he left without a word.

Catherine's head slowly dropped down into her folded arms on the table. Kissing Michael had drained the last bit of emotion out of her, and his leaving had taken her last bit of hope. Nothing could get them clear of this mess. Even Michael couldn't pull that off. She closed her eyes, her heart aching with pain, welcoming the oblivion of sleep.

# Chapter Ten

"Catherine, Catherine!"

Catherine struggled out of a deep sleep to see who was calling her. Her whole body began twitching, and with a start she opened her eyes and saw the familiar face of Marilyn leaning over her.

"Are you okay?" Marilyn inquired, her eyes clouded with concern.

"I... I think so," Catherine stammered, trying to clear her mind. "Where am I?"

"You're at the office," she informed Catherine gently. "It's seven-thirty in the morning."

"Oh, no." It all came back to her.

"Have you been here all night?" Marilyn inquired.

Catherine nodded gloomily, pushing her hair back from her face as she tried to stifle a yawn. She looked down at her rumpled red silk dress. "I must look awful."

Marilyn smiled. "Not at all. Maybe you're not at your usual peak of perfection, but still acceptable."

"Thanks," she said with a wry grimace. Then her eyes suddenly widened and she quickly looked around the room. "Where's Michael? Have you seen him this morning?"

"No, but I just got in a few minutes ago."

Where was he? What was the "plan" he had referred to? Where had he gone last night, and why wasn't he back yet? Catherine wondered frantically. She prayed he hadn't done something rash. No matter what happened to her job, she couldn't bear for anything to happen to him.

"If you don't mind me asking," Marilyn began in a hesitant voice, "what were you doing here all night?" Her eyes widened as if realizing what she was asking, and she added quickly, "Not that you have to tell me, of course."

Catherine gave a short, ironic laugh. "Nothing was going on here between Michael and me, if that's what you were thinking—nothing except a desperate search for something that would save my job."

"What?" Marilyn exclaimed.

Catherine sighed deeply and then began to relate the whole story of the missing funds and the all-night search for some piece of evidence to establish her own innocence.

"So the money disappeared through maintenance funding?" Marilyn asked.

"It seems so." The note of hopelessness was creeping back into Catherine's voice. "And since I'm the one who authorized the requisitions for maintenance, I'll have to take the responsibility for any figures that don't gibe between the budget and the actual expenditures."

Marilyn was silent for a few moments.

Catherine continued, "No matter what, the finger will point at me."

"Not necessarily," Marilyn interjected.

Catherine shook her head. "Marilyn, you know I'm the only one who signs those requisition forms—"

"Not *every* form."

"What are you talking about?"

"Some of those forms were signed by Bill Myers," Marilyn informed her matter-of-factly.

"What?" Catherine came up out of her chair and grabbed one of the requisition forms from the pile on the conference table. She took it over to her secretary and held it up in front of her face. "Do you mean some of these forms?"

"Yes, right."

Catherine seized Marilyn by the shoulders and riveted a wild-eyed glance on her. "You have to be very, very sure about this."

"I am," Marilyn said calmly. "Mr. Myers asked for maintenance requisition forms three times this year. He said it was on his authorization that the work was being done. He signed the forms and said not to bother you with any of the details, because you and he had already discussed it."

Catherine closed her eyes and said through gritted teeth, "That weasel. I can't believe I was so stupid."

"When the expenditures came through, I thought they were rather high, but I didn't think I should question you about it because you and Mr. Myers were...well...on friendly terms and you weren't—" She broke off and cast her eyes downward.

"The most approachable boss?"

"No, no," Marilyn hastened to assure her. "I just wasn't sure what to do. Mr. Myers is the executive vice-president, after all."

"I know." Suddenly aware of her iron grip on Marilyn's shoulders, Catherine dropped her hands and then patted Marilyn on the arm. "But I appreciate you coming forward now." Catherine tried to force her mind to start thinking coherently. Okay. Bill Myers was in on this budget fraud with Dr. Cramer. Of course. She should have suspected Bill. He always was a yes man who'd do anything to get ahead. Catherine grimaced inside at those words. How many times had she said those very words about herself?

No time for that now. She had to decide how to handle this. She had a witness in Marilyn, who could state that she'd seen Bill Myers signing requisition forms that were mysteriously high, but it was Marilyn's word against his. He would undoubtedly deny the whole thing. And he was a VP, while Marilyn was a secretary. Not good, but it was all Catherine had at this point. Maybe she and Marilyn could bluff their way through a confrontation with the president and Bill.

"Marilyn, would you be willing to go with me to present this information to the president this morning?" Catherine stopped suddenly, realizing what she was asking. "If you don't want to, I'd understand. Taking sides with me at this point could be bad for your career—depending on how it turns out."

"Of course I'll go with you," Marilyn answered without hesitation. "And I'll even bring my copies, even though—"

"What! You made copies of the forms?" Catherine almost shouted.

"I certainly did," Marilyn pronounced with a smug little smile. "Mr. Myers said not to bother keeping any records because he'd give the originals to you, but I made photocopies when he stepped out of the office."

Catherine turned her face upward and clasped her hands together in a prayer of thanks. "Marilyn, you're a genius. No, you're a saint, and if I come out of this with my whole skin, I'll remember who saved me."

"I was only doing my job. And besides, I hope you don't mind me saying this, but I never trusted Mr. Myers."

"You were smarter than I was about him, that's for sure." Catherine's voice hardened as the image of Bill rose in her mind. That lousy, scheming phony—pretending to actually care for her when he was really just setting her up. How could she have been so blind?

And to think she'd actually held it against Michael that he wasn't more like Bill. She almost laughed out loud at her own foolishness. Fancy clothes and a prestigious job didn't make the man, she realized with fearful clarity. It was integrity, honesty—all those qualities that Michael possessed in abundance.

*Oh, Michael, I'm sorry I've misjudged you,* she whispered to herself. *And please don't do anything that might get you in trouble,* she added.

Catherine checked her watch. It was almost eight. The president would be coming in soon, and she had to move into action now. "Marilyn, we've got to make our plans so we can get to Dr. Cramer as soon as he gets in this morning."

"What about Mr. Moreno?"

A pang of fear stabbed at Catherine's heart again. "He said he had another plan, but I'm not sure what it was or if it even worked out. So we'll just have to proceed, okay?"

Marilyn nodded and Catherine outlined what she had in mind.

An hour later, Catherine sat drumming her fingers on the armrests of a chair in the president's office. Marilyn was clenching and unclenching her hands in the chair next to Catherine. Both women kept glancing at the door, waiting for the president to make his entrance. They'd been sitting there for almost twenty minutes, and Catherine was ready to explode with the tension.

"Are you all right?" she asked Marilyn.

"I'm fine," Marilyn said in a tight voice. Her lips were pressed together in a thin line and only a muscle quivering in her jaw betrayed her anxiety. "We're doing the right thing."

"I know." Catherine paused and with a trace of irony in her voice continued, "I just don't know if it's the *smart* thing."

"Oh, it's not smart at all."

They exchanged sideways glances and then laughed nervously. At that moment, the door swung open and they were instantly silenced, expecting the president to walk in.

"Michael," Catherine cried in joy and surprise as she almost leaped out of the chair. But she abruptly slid back down when she saw Dr. Cramer and Bill Myers were following in his wake. She took a calming breath, her glance darting back and forth between Michael and the two men who followed him, trying to get a clue as to what was going on.

"Catherine, this is an unexpected surprise," Dr. Cramer pronounced as he walked around his massive mahogany desk. Then he frowned when he caught sight of Marilyn. "But what's your secretary doing here?"

"I asked her to be here for this discussion," Catherine responded in a firm voice.

Dr. Cramer settled comfortably into his leather chair and leveled a cool stare in Catherine's direction. "A discussion. That's interesting. I just met Mr. Moreno outside my office and he says he also has something to discuss with me." His glance shifted over to Michael. "I hope you two haven't been at each other's throats at the negotiating table and now want to request another negotiator."

Catherine almost burst into laughter at his assumption. Nothing could be further from the truth. She wouldn't mind spending the rest of her life with Michael.

She cleared her throat lightly. "Actually, Dr. Cramer—"

"No, Catherine, let me play the heavy," Michael cut in. "I've got a few questions for you that Ms. Walker wasn't able to answer—questions about the budget." He emphasized the last word deliberately and carefully.

The president's smile remained intact, but Catherine noted that he paled slightly under his tan.

"Really?" Dr. Cramer asked in a nonchalant tone.

Bill coughed lightly. "This doesn't concern me, so I'll go on back to my office and—"

"But this does concern you," Catherine interjected. Michael looked at her inquiringly, but she gave only the slightest nod of her head. "I think you'd better stay, Bill."

Bill hovered around the door for a few moments of indecision and then jammed himself into a seat. Catherine almost gloated as his brow wrinkled with worry.

"I think this situation calls for plain speaking, so that's what I'm going to do," Michael began as he set a folder on the desk in front of the president.

Catherine's heart thrilled as she watched Michael. In spite of his wrinkled suit, he radiated the self-confidence and poise of a man who was comfortable with himself no matter what the situation. Why hadn't she seen that before?

Michael continued. "In that folder is an analysis of the Palm City Community College budget. You'll find there's a two hundred thousand dollar discrepancy in the maintenance funds. That is, two hundred thousand dollars' worth of work was budgeted for maintenance, but there's no record anywhere else in the budget of this work having been done."

The president leaned back in his chair, his hands laced loosely in his lap. "You'll have to talk to Catherine. She's in charge of maintenance requisitions."

Michael nodded, an ironic grin crossing his face. "I thought you'd say that. So I did ask her about it last night. But, you know, the darndest thing is, she didn't have any record of that work being done either."

The president straightened up in his chair, concern crossing his face for the first time. "Catherine, do you mean to tell me that work was done at this college and you have no record of it?"

145

Catherine was silent, not sure what Michael was getting at.

"You realize, Catherine, that the college will have to conduct a full investigation if this money cannot be accounted for." Dr. Cramer's voice deepened with an authoritative edge.

He was good, Catherine had to admit. President Cramer was a born actor. And he played outrage especially well.

"Yes, I realize that," Catherine responded automatically.

"I don't think so," Michael interjected in a silky voice. "Because I've conducted my own investigation. This morning I spoke to Larry Andrews—the head of the maintenance company that the college uses—and he said that a lot of 'special' work has been done recently at your house, of all places." Michael paused. "To the tune of about two hundred thousand dollars—additions, a swimming pool, a tennis court— that kind of thing. Don't you think that's a little...well...coincidental?"

"Not at all," the president replied smoothly. "I've wanted to make those renovations for more than a year."

*He's got gall,* Michael had to concede. He'd seen some bald-faced liars in his time, but this man took the cake. "It'll be interesting to see how your personal financial statements gel with these huge sums spent on renovations."

"I don't have to release my financial records to you, Moreno," he replied softly, mockingly.

"Maybe not to me, but you'll have to give them up to the state attorney investigating this matter," Michael countered in an equally soft but threatening tone.

"Dr. Cramer—" Bill finally began to speak up.

"Shut up." The president silenced him with a flash of his steel-gray eyes.

Catherine almost grimaced at the way Bill visibly cringed under the menacing gaze of the president.

"You've not nothing on me, Moreno," Dr. Cramer murmured, spacing the words evenly, deliberately. "There's nothing to support your accusations. So get out of here and stop wasting my time."

Catherine saw Michael's hands clench into fists as he grated out, "I've only just started. Once we dig through your financial records you'll—"

"I don't think that's really necessary," Catherine cut in.

Michael stared at her, surprised by her interruption.

She spoke calmly. "I've got the requisition forms."

"What?" all three men said in unison.

"That's not possible." Bill's voice rose above the others.

"I'm afraid it is, Bill." She shot a cold glance in his direction. "Even though you told Marilyn not to keep copies of the forms, she made them anyway. And your signature is on three separate maintenance requisition forms adding up to, guess what? Two hundred thousand dollars."

"It wasn't my decision," Bill whined pathetically. "Dr. Cramer asked me to do it. The money went to *his* house, not mine."

"Shut up, you fool," Dr. Cramer shouted. "I should've known better than to get you into this. You're too much of an idiot to do anything right."

As he continued to vent his anger on Bill, Catherine felt almost nauseated. They were nothing but sleazy conartists. How could she have ever been so blind as to trust them? And to think she'd actually admired Dr. Cramer at one time and had worked like a dog at her job to win his approval.

"Okay, so what is it you want, Moreno?" the president finally snarled, all pretense of civility having gone out of his voice. "Money? Political favors?"

Michael shook his head and laughed in disbelief.

"Oh, I get it," Dr. Cramer spat out as he glanced in Catherine's direction. "You want an executive vice-presidency for that traitorous bit—"

"That's enough," Michael lashed out. "I know this is hard for you to believe, but not everybody thinks in terms of cutting deals."

"Really?" The president lifted one brow in contemptuous skepticism.

"No deals." Michael said shortly. "I'm afraid it's not up to me. The information will be turned over to the state attorney."

"What? My career will be ruined," Bill sniveled. "What am I going to do about my car payments? My mortgage? How will I get another job if this scandal—"

"I guess we all have to make choices, and you made yours," Michael said quietly.

"This is ridiculous. I just can't believe this," Bill exclaimed, wringing his hands. "My life is ruined. What am I going to do? Cathy, what am I going to do?" His eyes pleaded with her.

"I'm sorry, Bill." Catherine closed her eyes. A wave of weariness washed over her. She couldn't take much more. She was weary of the whole situation and she was weary of the people. Every illusion she'd held had been shattered in the last twenty-four hours and with it the life she'd so carefully constructed. "Michael, I think I'd like to leave now."

"Yes, you go on home. You had a rough night," he agreed in a gentle voice as he placed a reassuring arm on her shoulder. "I'll tie up the details and see you later."

"How touching," the president murmured sarcastically.

Michael opened the door for her and Marilyn to exit. As Catherine left, the image of the president's anger, Bill's pitiful despair, and Michael's triumph burned into her mind. At least she and Michael had beat them at their own game.

# Chapter Eleven

Hours later, Catherine lay on her bed staring up at the ceiling. She hadn't moved since she came home, dragged off her clothes, and threw herself on the bed. Utterly spent, she couldn't bring herself to get up, yet somehow she couldn't sleep either. So she just lay there, her mind spinning over the events of the morning again and again like a gyroscope, trying to make sense of it all.

One thing stood out: She had been wrong about everything. She had misjudged everyone. The people she had trusted had turned out to be dishonest, and the people she had distrusted turned out to be honorable and true to her. How could she have been so misguided? There wasn't one part of her preciously planned life that had turned out the way she had expected. She had followed all the ideas that her mother had hammered into her about pursuing her career and dating only ambitious men, and what had she ended up with? A life that was shallow and an ex-boyfriend who had betrayed her.

Catherine groaned and flung an arm across her face. And what about Michael? Had he stood by her just to prove something to himself? Or did he do it because he loved her?

She didn't know what to think. This certainly wasn't the way she'd expected things to turn out when she and Michael first started negotiating that contract. She never thought the people she worked for would turn out to be crooks. And she never dreamed she would fall in love with Michael.

What would happen next?

No matter how much she had feared the outcome of the events in the last twenty-four hours, she'd never felt the terrible emptiness that assailed her now when she tried to imagine her life without Michael. She'd treated him like a menial when she first met him and then kept trying to force him into conforming to her ideal of a professional man. But now she knew that no matter what he did or how he dressed, Michael was the man for her.

But did he want her?

"Cathy!" a voice shouted from outside.

Catherine slid off the bed and moved to her open window. As she peered outside, she saw Ruth standing under her window.

"Sorry, Cathy, but Shalimar ran under your house again and I can't reach her." She gestured toward the crawl space beneath Catherine's porch.

"I'll be right down." At least she could solve Ruth's problems. Her own were another story. She threw on an old pair of faded denim shorts and a pink T-shirt and then went out front to join Ruth.

"How in the world does that cat manage to get under there?" Catherine wondered aloud as she peered in the small opening at the base of her house. "These crawl spaces are to ventilate the house, not give cats a hiding place."

"Try telling Shalimar that," Ruth said wryly.

"I will if I ever get that little she-devil out of there." Catherine knelt down and then lay flat on her stomach. She squinted, her eyes trying to adjust to the dark recess under the house. "I think I see her."

Catherine stretched her arms out and slid in a wormlike motion under the house. She wrinkled her nose at the smell. It was dank and musty. "Ouch," she exclaimed as she scraped her knee on a piece of metal.

"Ruth, call to her," Catherine urged.

"Here, Shally," Ruth called out in a high-pitched voice.

"I don't believe this," Catherine muttered to herself. "After the morning I've had, this is the last thing I need."

As she slid in farther, she saw a flash of silvery-gray fur. She grasped at it and caught Shalimar by the tail. The cat whined, but Catherine held firm. She grabbed the cat's body with her other hand and then pulled her close.

"Okay, Shalimar, enough games," she warned as she started to slide back out from under the house, still holding the cat. But that proved to be impossible. She couldn't inch back out and still maintain a hold on Shalimar.

"Shoot," she exclaimed. "Ruth, you're going to have to pull me out."

Nothing happened. Catherine sighed in exasperation. "Ruth!" she shouted.

Two hands suddenly grasped her by the ankles and gently pulled. Catherine glided across the ground until she was clear of the crawl space. Once out, Shalimar twisted out of her grip and ran off. Catherine rolled over and sat up—only to find herself staring into Michael's dark eyes, now glinting with amusement. He had knelt down and was leaning back on his heels. His shirtsleeves were rolled up, revealing the strong arms that had just pulled her out of trouble.

"I guess having a blue-collar guy around the house comes in handy." His voice was gently mocking.

Catherine's breath caught in her throat. There was so much she wanted to ask him, but she found herself unable to speak. She could only cling to his eyes and hope that he could read the message in her heart.

151

"You have the tiniest streak of dirt on your cheek." Michael softly brushed the side of her face with his fingers and then smoothed back her hair.

"Is there something in my hair too?"

"No, I just wanted to feel your skin under my fingers." His voice had turned low and vibrant.

"Michael—" she began.

"What did you do to your knee?" He lifted her leg gently. "You cut it on something."

Catherine grimaced. "And now it's all dirty."

"Come on, let's go in the house and get it cleaned up."

Michael helped her to her feet and then scooped her into his arms and carried her up the front porch steps. He stopped when he saw Ruth across the yard holding Shalimar. "I see we both got what we were looking for." He winked at her.

"And about time," Ruth commented with a smile.

Catherine hid her face in Michael's shoulder so Ruth couldn't see her blush. "You don't have to carry me. I can walk on my own," she murmured against his shirt as he shoved open the front door with his shoulder.

"But I want to. I want to hold you and take care of you like this for the rest of my life." He tightened his arms. Then he continued in a pleasant voice, "Besides, I want to show you all the advantages of being with a guy like me. I'm strong, capable, and I can rescue you when little emergencies come up."

She tilted her head back. "Well, maybe you might come in handy."

Michael set her down on the kitchen counter and then dampened a towel to carefully clean away the dirt from her cut knee. "It's just a scratch, after all," he murmured as he softly dabbed it dry.

"Great." Catherine started to slide off the counter.

"Not so fast," Michael stopped her. Then he scooped her back up in his arms again. "I don't want to take a chance on your fainting after that *terrible ordeal* under the house." He carried Catherine into the living room and sat down in a large armchair, settling her on his lap.

"Michael, I'm okay, really," she protested, squirming in his arms.

Relenting, he opened his arms in a wide arc.

She started to move and then settled back onto his lap. "I don't feel like getting up now."

Michael laughed and folded his arms around her again. "You haven't asked me what happened after you left this morning."

"What? Oh, yes, with Dr. Cramer," she recalled with mild interest. Right now, all she could focus on was the fascinating interplay of muscles under Michael's white shirt.

"And Bill Myers," he reminded her.

"Bill who?" she said dreamily.

"Bill Myers."

"Oh, him, right." She reluctantly came back to reality. "Tell me what happened."

"Dr. Cramer and Myers both resigned. The information will go to the state attorney and there'll be a full investigation." He paused. "But I said I wouldn't go public with the information against them."

"Why not?" she asked in disbelief.

Michael shrugged. "I prefer to let the state attorney handle it. If the media gets hold of it now, without all the facts out in the open, the reporters will crucify them." His expression turned sober, and Catherine knew he was thinking about his own past. "There's no point in beating a man when he's down. Even if the investigation is low-key, Dr. Cramer and Myers will have to pay back the money and they sure won't be able to get administrative jobs anywhere else."

Once she realized what he was saying, Catherine's love and respect for Michael simply soared. He extended honor and compassion even to those who didn't deserve it.

"And by the way, that was a stroke of genius to find those requisition forms. I wouldn't have been able to pressure them into resigning so quickly without it."

"I can't take credit for it. Marilyn saved the day," Catherine pointed out frankly.

"A big thanks to her."

"And more."

"You can show her your appreciation when you take over as interim president," he said in a matter-of-fact voice.

"What?"

"You're the next senior administrator, so it falls to you until a formal search begins for a new president."

"But, Michael—"

"Then, if you want the job permanently, you can throw your hat in the ring and apply with the rest of the candidates." He smiled into her eyes. "I think you'd have a good chance."

Catherine's eyes gleamed as she imagined herself as president of the college. Top administrator before she was even thirty. What an accomplishment that would be for her. The prestige...the excitement. Then unconsciously her brow furrowed as she thought of the pressure, the late hours, the lack of time for herself...and Michael.

She looked at him, remembering what mattered most to her now. "I'll do it as an interim, but after that I want my old job back," she said firmly.

"Are you sure?" he asked softly. "This kind of chance doesn't come along every day, and if you don't take it, you might be vice-president for a long time."

Catherine shook her head. "I don't think so. When I said my old job, I meant teaching. It's been in the back of my mind for a long time, and when I took over Linda's class, I realized how much I missed being in the classroom again. I want to go back to teaching. It's where I was happiest and it's where *I* want to be."

She heard his quick intake of breath. "No, let me finish, Michael. I've had a lot of revelations this morning, not the least of which is what a fool I've been about a lot of things. But mostly I realized that I wasn't living my life. I was living the life my mother wanted for me. All those things I thought I was pursuing because I wanted them weren't true at all—I guess I was still trying to please her. She was always so concerned with status and security—not that I blame her. She just never felt she had enough. But I have to live my life and do what I want to do." She paused, gathering her nerve. "I want to teach. I want to have time for my friends and go to Little League games. And I want to be with you." Her voice broke off as a flash of shyness swept through her.

Michael grinned. This was what he'd been waiting for. He reached over and took one of her hands in his and lifted it to his cheek. "My sentiments exactly."

"Really?" Wonder touched her eyes as she stroked the side of his cheek with the back of her hand.

"Really. I want to live here with you—for always." His eyes captured hers, and the tenderness and passion she saw there made her catch her breath. "Don't you know how crazy I am about you? I have been since that moment I saw you at the gas station."

Catherine lowered her eyes, studying the buttons on his shirt intently. "I guess I overdid it a little," she murmured. "Ordering you around and everything."

He brushed her words aside with a wave of his hand. "I didn't come here to fall in love, believe me, Catherine. I wanted to settle that contract and clear out. But you stirred up feelings in me right from the start that I just couldn't ignore. I had to face up to all the old resentments about being the son of a migrant worker and the buried anger over losing my career. And then, even worse, was the fear that I wouldn't be able to keep you from losing your job." His voice turned deep and husky. "I would've done anything to protect you, Catherine."

"Katie."

He smiled.

"I love you, Michael."

A glint of wonder now touched his face as he cradled her face tenderly in his hands. "I love you too." Drawing her face toward his, his mouth touched hers, light as a summer breeze. But one touch rekindled all the pent-up emotion between them and they held each other tightly, rediscovering each other. His smooth cheek next to hers, the hard feel of his body against hers, his gently insistent mouth—it all felt so right to Catherine, except now there was almost a dreamy intimacy to his touch that she hadn't felt before.

Eventually, Michael drew back a little. "Oh, I forgot to tell you that I called the union this morning and said I was resigning after the contract was done."

"Are you sure?" Catherine exclaimed.

"I want to open a private practice again. It's time I set down roots. I want to marry you and live here with you. I want to coach Little League games with our children. And I want to spend the rest of my life showing you how much I love you."

Catherine's eyes filled with tears. "I don't know what to say." Marriage. Children.

He looked at her steadily, intensely. "Just say yes."

"Yes."

His mouth found hers again in a soul-rocking kiss. Then he suddenly drew back again and regarded her with a teasing smile. "But don't think this gets you off the hook with that contract."

"What?" she asked, puzzled. Her mind was dazed with the emotion of his kiss.

"We've still got a contract to settle," he reminded her as he started to nuzzle her neck.

Catherine closed her eyes, savoring the feel of his lips on her skin. "No concessions," she murmured.

"None?"

"Well...."

He nibbled her earlobe. "We should probably go back to work and get in a few hours of negotiating."

"You're right." Her arms slid around his neck.

"Or...you could give me the tour of the rest of the house."

Her laughter floated up from her throat in pure joy. "I think it's time for you to get the full tour."

"I intend to," he whispered as he rose and lifted her in his arms again, enfolding her in his warmth and love. "But it might take some time."

"We've got the rest of our lives."

# About the Author

**Martha Ambrose** is the author of a number of articles and short stories that have appeared in national publications. She divides her time between writing and teaching writing to college freshmen. A native of St. Louis, she now lives in Fort Myers, Florida, with her husband and their Himalayan cat.

Made in the USA
Lexington, KY
26 August 2018